Icarus Worl _____

Celebration:
Visions and Voices of
the African Diaspora

Series Editors, Roger Rosen and Patra McSharry Sevastiades

THE ROSEN PUBLISHING GROUP, INC.
NEW YORK

Published in 1994 by The Rosen Publishing Group, Inc.
29 E. 21st Street, New York, NY 10010

First Edition

Library of Congress Cataloging-in-Publication Data

Celebration : visions and voices of the African diaspora / series editors,
Roger Rosen and Patra McSharry Sevastiades.
        p. cm. — (Icarus world issues series)
    Includes bibliographical references and index.
    ISBN 0-8239-1808-4(hc):   —ISBN 0-8239-1809-2(pbk):
    1. Afro-Americans—History. 2. Afro-Americans—Biography.
    3.Afro-Americans—Fiction I. Rosen, Roger. II.Sevastiades, Patra
    McSharry. III. Series.
    E185.C44 1994
    973' .0496073—dc20   93-47413
                                                    CIP
                                                    AC

Manufactured in the United States of America

Contents

Introduction

The extraordinary power and influence of African culture in the Americas, and indeed throughout the world, has for far too long been either ignored or appropriated by the dominant culture which has in some measure been threatened by this other tradition. Celebration of the artistic achievements on the African continent and in the diaspora is long overdue. "Celebration: Visions and Voices of the African Diaspora" is a volume of voices that have joined with a rising tide of others to speak eloquently against an ignorance that racism, colonialism, and a slave-labor economy conspired to perpetuate from the sixteenth century to our own times.

That so many of the fruits of the diaspora should have been underground for so long is not difficult to fathom. Spawned in freedom in the motherland—where those self-same traditions live today as part of the fabric of daily life, transported across the Atlantic in chains in the hull of a slave ship, and practiced in secret in the inhospitable climate of a new land that denied every vestige of dignity, the culture of the diaspora has had an evolution akin to those species that have thrived in harsh climes, adapting, changing, and camouflaging in order to survive and be renewed.

To those stalwarts of the ancien régime who fume and froth at what they regard as a perverse fascination with "primitivism," "black magic," "drums and incantations," and "mumbo jumbo," the reply must be swift: It is only "a roughness of the eye," a bias of birth, a self-satisfied ignorance, and a pervasive fear that could send the Yoruba Orisha, the Brazilian *capoeiristas*, and the Mossi mask makers to the back of the bus. Using the Canon as a canon serves nobody's sense of inquiry. Tracing Paul Klee's figures back to the aesthetic vision of the Lega people or syncopations and cross-rhythms back to eastern Ghana and

western Togo, or certain constructions of insults (snaps)
back to the Ashanti does not prevent anyone from traveling on another day to Troy or stopping in Vinci or explor-
ing Persepolis. Why limit the itinerary?

African diaspora studies are in their infancy.
Practitioners of the arts and rituals have always abounded,
defending continuity against incredible odds, but only in
the past twenty or so years have qualified guides chosen
to come forth, seen fit to train others, to lead us through
the miraculous incarnation of sub-Saharan cultures in
Brazil, Cuba, the United States, and ultimately the rest of
the globe. *Icarus* is proud to offer a fascinating excursion
through breathtaking terrain. While student I.D.s will
ensure a window seat, everyone is guaranteed a seat at the
front of the bus.

Roger Rosen, Editor

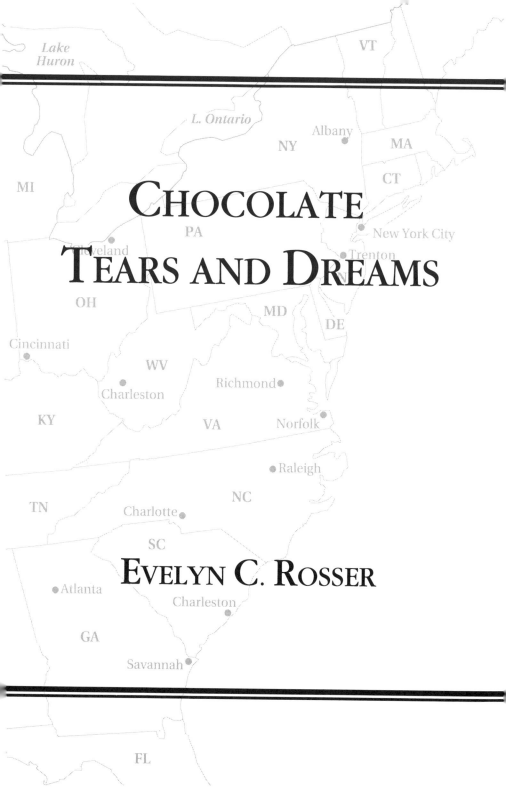

CHOCOLATE
TEARS AND DREAMS

EVELYN C. ROSSER

Evelyn Crawford Rosser was born in Valdosta, Georgia. She holds a Master of Education Degree in English.

Ms. Rosser was awarded first prize from the Southern Georgia Writer's Guild for her short story "There Will Be No Pain," and was the recipient of the Editor's Choice Award of the National Library of Poetry for her poem "Walls." Ms. Rosser's work has appeared in *Woman to Woman* and *The Anthology of Southern Poetry*, among other publications. Her forthcoming novel *Too Late for Tears* will be published by Dorrance in May.

Ms. Rosser lives in Athens, Georgia, where she is a high school English teacher and instructor in the Upward Bound program at the University of Georgia.

The following selection, comprising several diary entries from Ms. Rosser's childhood diary, is an excerpt from the forthcoming anthology *Life Notes: Personal Writings by Contemporary Black Women*, to be published in February by W. W. Norton.

*S*ummer 1952

I had fun today. My best friends, Shirlie and Alice, came to play with me. Mama told us to play outside. She had a cake in the oven, and didn't want it to fall. We played a game of make-believe. Shirlie was Elaine Stewart. Alice was Jane Russell. I was Marilyn Monroe! I lived in a beautiful house on the beach. Every evening I took my French poodle for a long walk. I loved to feel the sea breezes on my face and the surf gently lap against my feet.

Shirlie made me mad. She said I am chocolate, and everybody knows only white ladies have poodles and live on beaches. She said she could live on the beach, because she looks like Lena Horne. I started to cry. That's when Alice made Shirlie shut up. Alice said it didn't matter what color I was when I was born. I could bleach my skin. She knew it for a fact. Her cousin Betty did it. She used something called Black and White Ointment. She rubbed it on her face and neck every morning and night. Alice said the only problem was I couldn't let the sun strike me. Her cousin Betty never went outside without a hat or scarf on, 'cause if you do you'll turn blacker than you were before. I trembled at the idea. I'll miss playing with Shirlie and Alice, but I want to live in a fine house someday like the white ladies do. I'll ask God to speed up my bleaching.

Winter 1952

We spent the night sitting in Mama and Daddy's bedroom around the heater chewing cane and telling stories. Daddy's were the best. I enjoyed his stories, but he made me scared to go to bed. I think I'll sleep with the cover over my head tonight. I hope I don't dream about the headless woman walking down the railroad track or the horse that wouldn't move unless the rider gave him a drink of moonshine. Sometimes I think Daddy makes these stories up.

He ended the night by telling about the end-of-the-year program in Douglas, Georgia. Daddy lived out in the country on a farm called Huffas. To get her teaching contract renewed the teacher had to have her students entertain the superintendent and board of education members at the end of the school term. Daddy said he was in a skit about slavery.

He loved to tell this part. Daddy got up from his chair and acted out the rest of the story for us. He said he wore a straw hat and overalls with one shoulder strap hanging down. He was barefooted. All the students were lined up in rows of fives, holding rusty hoes in their hands.

The guests sat quietly staring in anticipation. The teacher waved to the pianist to start the program. Daddy said the students started moving slowly, pretending to chop cotton.

They sang slowly and mournfully:

> "Mas told me
> Mas told me
> To stay on
> The old plantation."

At this point in the skit, each student took a handkerchief from his back pocket and wiped his face. The song continued:

> "Lord I'm tired
> Lord I'm tired
> Of this heavy
> Load I keep a-totin'
> Totin', totin'."

Then he said they began to chop wildly and move fast down the rows in the imaginary cotton field singing:

"Oh, a nigger sho knows
How to make things grow
By marchin' down the rows
And choppin' with a hoe."

The guests started yelling, "Ye ha! Well done, Miss Caroline. Best program ever!" Daddy said Miss Caroline's face beamed with satisfaction. She knew she had her job for another year.

The fire left Daddy's eyes as suddenly as it had appeared. He looked sad. He mumbled something about it being wrong for her to use them like that. Daddy said, "Negroes shouldn't use other Negroes to get what they want." I didn't know what he meant, but I knew something bad had happened to Daddy. Almost in a whisper he told us to go to bed. It hurt me to see Daddy sad. I'll sleep with the quilt over my head tonight. That way no one will hear me cry.

Winter 1952

I loved the doll I got for Christmas. Daddy broke it today. You see, it was an accident. My brothers took my doll from me and were throwing it back and forth to each other. When I ran to one brother, he threw it to another brother. I told Daddy to make them give it to me. He came into the bedroom and told them to stop throwing my doll. They didn't. He got angry. He snatched it from my brother and threw it to me. I didn't catch it. The doll hit the trunk. Its head was broken off. I cried. Daddy promised to buy me another doll. Mama told me to stop crying, because a nine-year-old girl was too old for dolls anyway. She said dolls only make girls want babies. She doesn't know me. I don't want a baby. I want a mink coat, a red convertible, and a big house on the beach. I'll have a funeral for my doll tomorrow, and I won't invite her.

5

Summer 1953

Today my brothers and I went to the movies. Last week Dick Tracy was trapped in a well. I had to know whether he got out alive. On the way to the movies, we noticed a new ice cream parlor. My brother Sonny said we had enough money to buy a five-cent cone each. Edward wanted strawberry. Sonny wanted vanilla. I wanted chocolate.

A teenage white girl was standing behind the counter. When we reached the counter, she walked away. She busied herself cleaning a table. We stood at the counter and waited for her to finish cleaning the table. She turned her head to look at us and started wiping the table again. By that time my brother Sonny was mad. He knocked hard on the counter several times. The girl didn't turn around. Sonny knocked again, this time louder. The girl ran from the room. A mean-looking man came out, drying his hands on a stained apron. "What do you want?" he yelled at us. "We want some ice cream," my brother answered. The man just stared at him. "I mean we want to buy some ice cream," added my brother. The man continued to stare. Then he said, "We don't serve niggers here!" He walked away, leaving us alone at the counter.

My brother Sonny wanted to jump across the counter and smash his face in. I begged him not to. I could do without the ice cream. We went to the movies, but I had a hard time keeping my mind on Dick Tracy. Today was the first time someone has ever called me a nigger to my face. Mama was right, I'm getting too old to play with dolls. There are more important things to think about.

Winter 1953

Mrs. W. died today. Actually, she was killed accidentally. Her husband is a mechanic. She loved to tinker with cars. Her car couldn't start so she pulled up the hood and tried to start it. I don't know all the details, or the technical terms to describe what happened, but when the motor cranked, the car took off by itself. It plowed into her house, crushing her to death. I pretended to be sad, but I wasn't. I didn't like her. She was the only person who made me feel ugly and unwanted since the ice cream parlor owner called me a nigger.

She broke my heart when I was eight years old. Shirlie, Alice, and I were playing outside during lunch. Mrs. W. beckoned for us to come to her. When we reached her, she looked at me and said, "Not you, just these two."

She took Alice and Shirlie into her classroom. She was giving a birthday party for a student in her class. I peeped inside the window. Alice was standing beside her licking a cone of ice cream. Shirlie was sitting on her lap, kicking her legs happily and enjoying a cone of ice cream. Mrs. W. was playing with Shirlie's hair. I decided Mrs. W. must have thought I was a nigger too and couldn't enjoy ice cream.

Spring 1954

I played, "That's What Dreams Are Made Of," over and over tonight. I hope I don't wear it out. I'm so happy. I was kissed by a boy for the first time! There's a dark hall in our school. When the lights go out it's pitch black. Well, the lights went out today. It was only for a few minutes, but Timothy kissed me. We closed our eyes and pressed our lips together. I must admit I was a little disappointed. My toes didn't curl, nor did I hear bells the way the ladies do in the *True Confession* magazines. I must not be doing something right, but I'm going to keep practicing every chance I get. I want to hear bells and see stars.

Fall 1955

Old Acid Tongue did it again! She picks a new student out every day to burn. Today was my lucky day. I wore the new dress my grandmother ordered for me from Belles Hess. I met the postman every day for six weeks! My dress is so pretty. It has a short cape that makes me think of Sherlock Holmes. I like to imagine myself living a mysterious life.

Well, anyway, I walked into Mrs. Tatum's room eager to show off my beautiful red dress. As soon as I stepped into the room, Old Acid Tongue lit into me. "How could your mother let you out of the house looking like that?" she asked. I looked behind me. I thought she was talking to someone else, but she kept staring at me.

"I'm talking to you in the red dress!" she shouted. I wanted to tell her that that was my dress and I could wear any color I wanted. Besides, that wasn't just any old red dress. It was the dress my grandmother had ordered for me, and I had filled out the order form! I didn't say anything, because I had seen her shake students for talking back to her. Whenever you try to explain yourself, you get deeper and deeper into a hole, and Old Acid Tongue just pours more acid on you. I didn't want the school to burn down!

Good Lord, Mrs. Tatum can fuss! She went on and on explaining why I shouldn't wear red. She even "for your own good" threw in a few extra colors—yellow, purple, and orange. She also cautioned me to stay away from some shades of brown. According to Mrs. T. I am chocolate, and brown does not complement my color. Within a few minutes Old Acid Tongue had eliminated four colors from my wardrobe.

I'll be glad when this school term comes to an end. I'll stay inside all summer and bleach my skin.

Spring 1956

Tonight was my shining hour. It was even better than when I was crowned Miss Pine Grove Junior High during the homecoming festivities. I delivered the first honor student's speech at our eighth-grade graduation exercises. The subject was "The Night Brings Out the Stars." I didn't understand the part about the night being a more familiar friend to me than man, but I didn't tell Mrs. S. She says I'm precocious and should go far in life. I asked her what precocious meant. She said that means I know more than I should at my age. I figure she knows what she's talking about, because I do my brother's homework. He's four grades ahead of me.

Anyway, I was real good tonight. Everybody said so. Mama and Daddy were smiling proudly. I know I'll forget most of the speech, but I wrote down my special part: "It is the dark hours of life that teach us to discriminate between the true and false, the fair-weather friends, and the faithful comrades." I'll have to remember that when I'm filthy rich, famous, and living in California.

Summer 1956

Daddy preached his trial sermon today. Mama didn't go to church with us, so I had to be her stand-in. I didn't like being the center of attention, but I was happy to be able to help my daddy. He has wanted to be a minister since he was a little boy. The deacons wanted to know where Mama was. Daddy told everyone Mama was sick. She really wasn't. Daddy had been drinking the night before, and she said he ought not play with God that way. Daddy had argued that there was nothing wrong with taking a little nip as long as you didn't hurt anyone. Mama still refused because she said she didn't want to see Daddy preach his own damnation. I could never picture Daddy in hell because he is a good man.

I knew Daddy was going to be all right from the moment he outlined his hymn. "Father I stretch my hands to thee, no other help I know. If thou withdrew thyself from me, O whither shall I go." The words dripped like honey from his lips.

When I looked at the congregation, smiling old ladies were fanning and moving their heads from left to right. A few raised their fans toward heaven and shouted, Yes, Lord! Hallelujah! My mind wandered to the food that would be spread out on the tables under the shade trees. I could pick what I wanted to eat, and I was going to eat lots of chocolate cake. By the time Daddy gave his text, he had the congregation eating out of his hands. "I am He," shouted Daddy, strutting across the pulpit like a proud rooster. When he got to the part about being Alpha and Omega, an old woman began to shout. She raised both hands into the air and spun around repeatedly. On one of her spins, her wig flew off. She stopped shouting, stooped down, picked up her wig and quietly sat down. She did not raise her head again until Daddy's sermon was over.

At the end of the sermon everybody congratulated Daddy and me. I didn't see that I had done anything of significance, but Daddy said I had saved the day for him. I felt a little guilty because I had winked at several boys while I pretended to be wrapped up in Daddy's sermon. If you ask me, Mama should have been sitting in the chair facing the altar. She was the one who vowed to God to love, cherish, honor, and obey Daddy, not me. I'm just a child. Besides I wouldn't marry a preacher anyway. Preachers' wives can't smoke or drink. If I'm going to live in California, I'll have to have champagne parties and smoke cigarettes in long fancy holders like the ladies do in the movies.

Spring 1957

Dear God, please teach me forgiveness. I was wronged today and I responded bitterly. I've grown accustomed to seeing "For Whites Only" signs on public facilities, sitting in the balcony in movie theaters, being served in the kitchen in restaurants, and sitting in the rear on buses. I'm used to being mistreated by white folks, but how do I deal with discrimination within my own race?

I was proclaimed the best speller in the school this year.

To get this honor, I sacrificed many hours of recreational time. Whenever I jumped rope or played hopscotch with my playmates, I would mentally spell words to a rhythmic beat. I was obsessed with one idea—bringing the first-place trophy for being the best speller in the district home to my high school.

However, I did not get the opportunity to compete in the district spelling bee today. A new girl named Katie had moved to town after I had won the intraschool competition. Her father is a principal, and her mother is a teacher. In contrast, my mother substitutes and works in the school lunchroom. My father preaches and works at a local lumberyard.

When I got to school this morning, Mrs. S. told me that I would not be the one to represent our school at the district spelling bee. She explained to me that she, along with other teachers, had decide that Katie would have a better chance to win the spelling bee because of her family's academic background. She further explained that I was culturally disadvantaged. I asked her what she meant by this. She said I had not been exposed to many books and had not traveled extensively. I told her I bet I had read more books from the school's library than anyone else in the school. She said that didn't count. The decision had been made.

I tried not to cry, but tears trickled down my face. Lord, I tried not to be disrespectful, but I had studied so hard. When I cried about the months I had wasted studying, Mrs. S. just patted me on the back and said, "Now dear, we must not think that way. No learning is ever wasted!"

In my frustration and anger, I wanted to slap her; but most of all, I wanted Katie to lose the spelling bee. After all, she had not earned the right to compete in the first place. I had! She had stolen my opportunity to be a winner.

Mrs. S. allowed me to attend the spelling bee. I sat alone feeling dejected, thinking about how my mother had sacrificed her money and time to dress me for the occasion. She had made a beautiful skirt and blouse for me at night,

11

after cooking and washing dishes all day. I knew my disappointment would break her heart more than it did mine.

I sat anxiously with fingers crossed, praying for Katie to lose. When she misspelled the word chrysanthemums during the second round, I cried tears of joy. Sweet vengeance was mine.

Please help me to understand what happened today. Help me to understand why I feel so rotten. I felt inferior today with my own race. Lord, help me to understand what this incident was trying to teach me.

Dear God, help me to become Katie's friend. She didn't have anything to do with what happened today. Give me the strength to keep on pursuing my dreams. Obsess me with fiery passion to succeed. Give me the courage to face life unafraid.

Dear God, bless my mama too. Help her to forgive my teacher. Mama called her tonight. She didn't apologize for what happened to me. Perhaps she thinks the incident is trivial. Perhaps she does not realize that children have feelings too. Perhaps she does not know that culturally disadvantaged people can be heartbroken too. When will she learn?

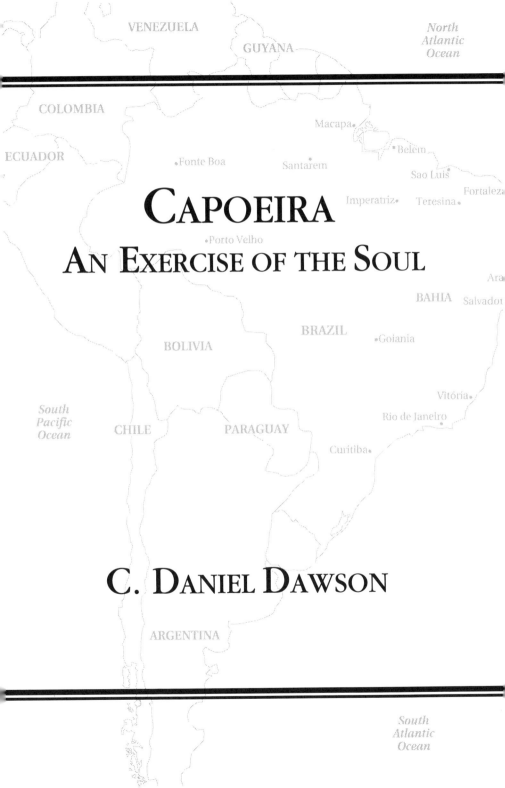

CAPOEIRA
AN EXERCISE OF THE SOUL

C. DANIEL DAWSON

C. Daniel Dawson studied filmmaking in New York City at the School of Visual Arts, the WNET Black Journal Training Program, and the New York University Graduate Institute of Film and Television. He taught filmmaking at the Studio Museum in Harlem, and while there was the first to initiate film festivals and photographic exhibitions. He returned to university to study philosophy, Eastern religions, and African art and culture. Returning to the Studio Museum, he became the first James Van Der Zee curator of photography, film, and video. He produced numerous international film festivals and mounted several photographic exhibits, some of which toured Asia and the Far East.

Mr. Dawson has been a producer/director of photography and sound recordist. He has produced documentaries and feature films. He collaborated on many award-winning films including "Head and Heart" by James Mannas and "Capoeiras of Brazil" by Warrington Hudlin. He was the director of special projects at the Caribbean Cultural Center, where he developed all of the Center's exhibitions. He has been the curator of more than thirty exhibitions over the last twenty years.

Mr. Dawson currently works as an arts and media consultant. He frequently lectures on African and African Diaspora cultures. He lives in New York City.

The Atlantic slave trade, sometimes known as the Middle Passage, wrought havoc on the cultures and political states of Africa and led to the forced migration of millions of Africans to the Americas. The Africans could not bring their material cultures and artifacts, but most important, they brought their histories and cultures—philosophies, languages, political structures, and religious and artistic expressions.

Hundreds of societies were established throughout the Americas by Africans who had freed themselves. These societies were called *maroons* in the United States, *palenques* in the Spanish-speaking countries, and *quilombos* or *mucambos* in Brazil. The most famous *mucambo* was the Quilombo dos Palmares, which existed for almost one hundred years as an independent republic made up of Africans, Native Americans, and poor whites. Many of these societies had their own system of self-defense or martial arts which, not surprisingly, had their origins in Africa.

Africans practiced a variety of martial arts. In the past, these techniques were usually practiced by young male warriors, but in a few cases like the ancient Kingdom of Dahomey and Angola women were also warriors. Higher, more magical techniques were secret knowledge that was guarded by a council of elders and taught only after strenuous initiations into warrior societies. From the top of northern Africa to the bottom of southern Africa there were and still are hundreds of fighting styles that emphasized skill, technique, and intelligence over brute force. One of the martial arts that sprang from these, *capoeira angola*, is still played in Brazil today.

As its name suggests, the search for the origins of *capoeira angola* should start in Angola. Albano de Neves e Souza of Angola wrote in an old letter that "*N'golo* is *capoeira."* Albano described *n'golo* as an acrobatic zebra dance performed by young males of the Mucope people of Angola. The dance had an aspect of competition: The man chosen as the best dancer was permitted to select a wife without having to pay the bride's family a marriage fee. The late Vincente Pastinha, the famous *capoeira angola* master of Brazil, stated that his own teacher, a man from Angola named Benedito, told him that *capoeira* was developed from the *n'golo* dance. Other references suggest different origins, although still from the same area in Central Africa. Mário Barcelos wrote in *Aruanda*, "Next to the Cambindas, there existed another people that played capoeira. They were the Mazingas, of the Congo, that were the eternal adversaries of the Cambindas in that art." Angola has other martial arts such as *njinga, basula,* and *gabetula.* These are considered forms that are similar to *capoeira angola* and helped create it. Add all the sources together: the *n'golo* dance, the art of the Mazingas and the Cambindas, the other martial dances of Angola, and you come to the general conclusion that *capoeira angola* began in Central Africa and traveled to Brazil as an already formed art, a fusion of the elements of dance, music, theater, and ritual. *Capoeira* may have evolved once it arrived in Brazil, but its origin is African.

Capoeira traveled with the Atlantic slave trade to Brazil, where it became an outlaw art. Legend has it that *capoeira* was used by Africans to fight slavery and oppression in the Portuguese colonial society. During the time of slavery the practice of *capoeira* was punishable by death. But the Brazilian government was finally forced to recognize the fighting skills of *capoeiristas,* as practitioners are called; in their war with Paraguay in the 1860s the *capoeiristas* served as front-line troops. More than 65,000 Afro-Brazilians died in that war.

After the abolition of slavery in 1888 *capoeira* continued as an outlaw art form, but by then it had become a part of

Brazilian society. It was practiced by Africans, Europeans, and those of mixed heritage, with the exception of the upper classes. At this time, *capoeira* was also used as an intimidation tactic. Roving bands of *capoeristas* were employed by politicians to intimidate opponents and by businessmen to put the competition out of business. In addition, it was the art of the hustlers and petty thieves who hung out in the streets of Salvador, Bahia, and Rio de Janeiro; their favorite weapon was a straight razor or a dagger. Even today the legacy of associating *capoeira* with crime can be found in the *Novo Michaelis Illustrated Dictionary* of 1983, which defines *capoeira* as a "criminal technique of sudden, violent assault, characterized by agile movement of the body." The negative view of *capoeira* is further complicated by the history of racial conflict and class politics in Brazilian society: *Capoeira* was marginalized in part because it was commonly identified with black and poor people.

In the twentieth century *capoeira* has become an acceptable part of mainstream Brazilian culture and is acknowledged as a national sport.

The *jogo-de-capoeira*, or play of *capoeira*, takes place at a *roda* (pronounced HO-da), a *capoeira* party at which *capoeiristas* gather to play. The players and onlookers form a circle, also called a *roda*. At the "top" of the circle is an ensemble of musicians and singers, known as the *bateria*.

Capoeira is rarely played without music. Music is one of the most important elements of the art, creating the atmosphere in which *capoeira* is most beautifully expressed. Music inspires the *capoeiristas* to more intense levels of interaction and is also used to calm them down when the game becomes too heated.

The *berimbau*, a bow with one string, is the most important musical instrument associated with *capoeira*. Attached to the bow is a hollowed gourd or *cabaça* that acts as a resonator box. Tones are produced when the bowstring is struck by a thin flexible stick, the *baqueta*. The hand that holds the *baqueta* also holds a small rattle, or *caxixi*. With its hypnotic sound, the *berimbau* is considered "the soul of *capoeira*."

In traditional *capoeira angola* schools, the musicians are placed in a particular order. One sees, from left to right: a *ganza* or *reco-reco*, a notched length of bamboo or a notched gourd played by scraping with a thin stick; an *agogô*, a double-headed bell struck with a stick or thin metal rod; a *pandeiro*, a tambourine; a *berimbau-gunga*, the *berimbau* with the largest gourd, which maintains the rhythm; a *berimbau-centro*, a *berimbau* with a mid-sized gourd, which also maintains the rhythm; a *berimbau-viola*, the smallest *berimbau*, which "speaks," that is, improvises the rhythms; a second *pandeiro*; and an *atabaque*, a drum played with the hands, similar to a conga drum. The dominant instruments are the three *berimbaus*; no other instrument should be played louder than they are. The types and use of songs also have an established order. In all, music is one of the most enriching aspects of *capoeira*.

The ritual of *capoeira* begins when two players enter the circle and kneel at the foot of the *berimbaus*. Still kneeling, one player sings a ritual song of commencement accompanied by the musicians. If his opponent does not respond with a song of his own, he begins a second song, a song for going out to play. The song is then passed on to one of the musicians, who continues singing it as the *joga-de-capoeira* begins.

A *capoeira* game is characterized by dynamic movements: cartwheels, handstands, spinning kicks, and spontaneous acrobatics. At its highest level, *capoeira* is considered an improvisational conversation between two bodies. This sensibility is very similar to a jazz performance. As *capoeira* scholar Kenneth Dossar writes in the *Afro-Hispanic Review*:

The object of the game is for the *capoeiristas* to use finesse, guile, and technique to maneuver one another into a defenseless position, rendering them open to a blow, kick, or sweep. Only one's hands, head, and feet are allowed to touch the floor. Being swept and landing on one's bottom disqualifies a player. In general, there is no contact from strikes. An implied strike is more admired . . .

Capoeira utilizes few offensive hand techniques. Some attribute this to the belief that slaves had to fight with their hands in chains and therefore emphasized foot and leg techniques. It is more likely, however, that the absence of hand techniques is based on an ancient Kôngo tradition in which hands should be used for good work, that is, creative activities, whereas feet should be used for bad work—punishment and destruction. Bakongo scholar Dr. K. Kia Bunseki Fu-Kiau recalls a relevant proverb in Kikongo, *Mooko mu tunga, malu mu diatikisa* (Hands are to build, feet are to destroy).

African practices tend not to separate parts of the culture into isolated and differentiated activities. *Capoeira* is no exception. Scholar Dr. Alejandro Frigerio writes, "*Capoeira* . . . is a multiform phenomenon: it is dance, fight, game, ritual and musical performance. It is a person's way of defense, and it is also a form of entertainment." It is based on African and Afro-Brazilian values. Dr. Frigerio identifies six elements intrinsic to modern *capoeira angola*: *malicia*, complementation, beautiful movement, slow rhythm, ritual, and theatrical aspects.

Malicia is the art of being tricky or deceptive. In the Afro-United States it is called "tricknology" or "oky doke." One aspect of *malicia* is to look vulnerable until the opponent attacks, then gracefully defend and/or counter-attack. One should play closed, while appearing open.

When playing *capoeira* one plays *with*, not *against*, the opponent; this has been described as complementation. It is similar to a "cutting session" in jazz in which the musicians try to outplay each other, the ultimate goal being the creation of beautiful music. Good *capoeira angola* is created with a flowing movement that produces the most creative interaction possible, limited only by the skills of the players.

It is not enough merely to "beat" the opponent; one must prove superior skill by displaying it with style, or beautiful movement. This is true for almost all African-American participation in sports including soccer, basketball, and boxing. Many sports commentators have misunderstood the black athlete and accused him of "showboating" or "hot-dogging," when in reality the athlete was manifesting an African aesthetic concerning beautiful movement.

The movement of *capoeira angola* generally has a slow and deliberate rhythm. As in many Chinese and Indian martial arts systems, if one can execute a movement slowly and perfectly, one can also execute it quickly and effectively.

Capoeira angola is a sophisticated ritual. If a player displays ignorance of these traditional, unwritten rules, he is considered an inferior player.

The *jogo* or play is performed before a group of spectators. Viewers should be entertained by the skill, deception, and humor of the play.

None have exhibited these six elements more skillfully than the two most famous modern masters, Mestre Bimba and Mestre Pastinha, who shaped the development of modern *capoeira*.

Mestre Bimba (1899–1979) was born Manoel dos Reis Machado in the Brotas section of Salvador. He was first taught to fight by his father, a champion *batuque* fighter. *Batuque* was an African-based martial dance also found in Brazil and similar to *capoeira*. At the age of twelve, Bimba was introduced to *capoeira* by Bentinho, an African from Angola who worked as a ship's captain for the Navigation Company of Bahia. Having learned it, Bimba became its great innovator. He combined elements of *batuque, capoeira,* and free-style fighting to create what he called *capoeira regional: a luta biana* (a Bahia fight). Bimba, a great singer, was also the best fighter of his time, a champion who faced all challengers and never lost a match. A large powerful man, he liked to fight, so it is not surprising that *capoeira regional* stressed the fighting aspect and de-emphasized the African cultural elements, which Bimba viewed as superfluous.

Bimba opened a public academy in 1927. In 1937 it became the first *capoeira* academy to be registered with the Brazilian government. But Brazilians could attend the academy only if they had a job or were in school. These restrictions prevented enrollment by almost all black Brazilians. Bimba wanted to change the image of *capoeira* by encouraging middle- and upper-class Brazilians to par-ticipate in it. Ultimately, embraced by the most influential classes of society, declared legitimate by government offi-cials, and featured in numerous newspaper articles, *capoeira regional* became famous throughout the country.

Despite the success of *capoeira regional,* Bimba did not receive much financial gain. He died broke and bitter. *Capoeira regional* was the most popular *capoeira* style in Brazil, but it no longer contained its deep cultural roots. Meanwhile, *capoeira regional* was changed even more by Bimba's students after his death.

The other legendary modern *capoerista* was Mestre Pastinha (1889–1981). Born Vincente Ferreira Pastinha, he played *capoeira* for more than eighty years. His father was a Spaniard, his mother, an African; and like Bimba he was taught *capoeira* by an African from Angola, Mestre Benedito. Benedito had seen the ten-year-old Pastinha, who was very small in stature, being beaten by a stronger boy. Afterward, he offered to teach Pastinha something very valuable. Benedito was, of course, talking about *capoeira angola,* or *n'golo* as he also called it. Pastinha was a brilliant *capoeirista*

21

whose game was characterized by agility, quickness, and intelligence. Whereas Bimba was the great innovator, Pastinha was the great traditionalist. Pastinha wanted his students to understand the practice, philosophy, and tradition of pure *capoeira angola*. As he said:

> I practice the true *capoeira angola* and in my school they learn to be sincere and just. That is the Angola law. I inherited it from my grandfather. It is the law of loyalty. The *capoeira angola* that I learned—I did not change it here in my school . . . When my students go on they go on to know about everything. They know: this is fight, this cunning. We must be calm. It is not an offensive fight. *Capoeira* waits . . .

One of Pastinha's students, Mestre João Grande (João Oliveira do Santos), was born on January 15, 1933, in the tiny village of Itagí in the southern part of Bahia. His journey from the backwoods of Brazil to New York City was neither short nor easy. His birthplace is so small that it does not appear on state maps.

Most of Itagí's inhabitants eked out a living as farm laborers receiving subsistence wages. The family of João Grande was no different. For little João there was no time for school or even play; it was all hard work. But he lived in the countryside, so it was easy for him to engage in his favorite pastime, studying nature. He was fascinated by the movement of trees in the wind, waves in the ocean, and especially the movements of animals, like the strike of a snake and the flight of a bird. João studied them with dedication. This was to have great influence on his practice and philosophy of *capoeira*. In fact, his first and only master, Mestre Pastinha, would later give him the nickname *Gavião* (Hawk) because of the manner in which he swept down on an opponent like a bird of prey. But João's father didn't appreciate his young son's activities; he wanted him to spend more time working. It was a difficult life.

Mestres João Grande and Pastinha.

At the age of ten João saw a *capoeirista* demonstrating a movement called *corta' capim* (cut the grass). It is performed by crouching down, extending one leg, and swinging it in a rotary motion under you. Each time the swinging leg approaches the crouching leg, you hop. This allows the swinging leg to continue its circular course uninterrupted. Fascinated by the movement, he was told it was "the dance of the Nagôs," black people in the city of Salvador roughly 825 miles away, in the state of Bahia. To people of the countryside like João, all people of African descent in Salvador were Nagôs or Yorubas. But the dance was actually of Central African origin; it was *capoeira*. João didn't learn its correct name until many years later. At the age of ten he left home in search of "the dance of the Nagôs."

João worked and walked his way through the countryside, seeking the intriguing dance. He eked out a living on the plantations and farms of Bahia. After ten years of slow travel, he was taken to Salvador by the family with whom he was living. João was now twenty years old and in the epicenter of *capoeira*, but he didn't know what it was called or where it could be found. Each day was full of ill-paid but hard labor. One day he was sent to *Roça do Lobo* (Clearing of the Wolf), a famous site for *capoeira*. Approaching the large crowd, he could see only the tops of sticks waving in the center. It was a *capoeira roda* with the *berimbau* sticks dancing in rhythm to the music. It wasn't just a run-of-the-mill street *roda*: It was a meeting of the important *capoeira* personalities, including João Pequeno, who was there with Mestre Barboza.

An enthralled João asked Mestre Barboza what this game was called and was told, "That is *capoeira*!" João asked where he could learn it. Mestre Barboza sent him to João Pequeno, who then sent him to Mestre Pastinha. Pastinha had a famous academy in Brotas, and his *rodas* were full of the most famous names in *capoeira*. This was *capoeira* heaven. At the age of twenty, João requested permission to join Pastinha's academy.

Mestre Pastinha accepted João as a student, which had a profound effect on João. As João stated, "Pastinha was my father, my grandfather, my everything in *capoeira*." At the academy, João Pequeno, who is now the oldest master still teaching, became his lifelong friend.

João Grande (Big John)—so called because he was bigger than his friend João Pequeno (Little John)—was again studying and working. Like many other *capoeiristas*, he worked as a stevedore in Salvador's port by day. It was a back-breaking job to unload heavy sacks from the boats. An exhausted but happy João studied *capoeira* at night in Pastinha's academy. João Grande was fast becoming one of the most respected *capoeiristas* in Bahia. Few would play him in street *rodas* for fear of being publicly embarrassed.

João Grande was so highly appreciated that when Carybé, a painter famous for his documentation of African culture in Bahia, wanted to do studies of *capoeira* he chose João Grande as the model. João Grande and João Pequeno also displayed their skills in numerous films, including one in which they showed the knife techniques of the art. In 1966 Pastinha took João Grande with him to demonstrate *capoeira* in Senegal at the first International Festival of Black Arts.

João was awarded his Diploma of *Capoeira* from Pastinha in 1968, making him a full-fledged master. In 1973 he toured Europe and the Middle East. He was now one of the symbols of *capoeira* in Bahia. In addition to playing *capoeira*, he also taught at Pastinha's academy.

As the years passed, all did not go well at the academy. Pastinha—old, sick, and almost totally blind, was asked by the government to vacate the building in which the academy was housed. The space had been donated to Pastinha by the government, which now wanted to renovate it. Once the improvements were completed, however, the space was not returned to Pastinha. It became a training restaurant with an amphitheater and was used as a school for cooks, waiters, dancers, musicians, and others in the field. Eight years later, Pastinha died, broke and bitter about his treatment by the government, but he had never expressed regret for having lived a life of *capoeira*.

Some years later, Mestre Pastinha finally received the recognition he deserved. In a brochure celebrating his 100th birthday the state of Bahia, Brazil, declared him part of the Heritage of Bahia.

Following Pastinha's death, João Grande dropped out of the *capoeira* world. He made a living working by day at a gas station and by night performing as a dancer and musician in a folkloric show for tourists. There he did not demonstrate *capoeira*. His producers wanted to see the flashy, acrobatic *capoeira regional* developed by Bimba. They didn't understand or appreciate the more complex and subtle game of *capoeira angola* played by João.

During this period, Mestre Moraes (Pedro Morales Trinidade), who had been João Grande's prize student, returned to Bahia after almost a decade spent in Rio de Janeiro. Moraes brought with him one of his top students, Cobrinha Mansa, who was now also a master. Moraes and Cobrinha founded Grupo de Capoeira Angola–Pelourinho (GCAP), an institution dedicated to continuing the work of Pastinha, João Grande, and the other great masters. GCAP initiated international conferences and demonstrations of *capoeira angola* and they brought together old masters to talk about the history and practice of the art. These conferences led to a revival of *capoeira angola* in Bahia. Moraes, Cobrinha, and GCAP wanted to educate the public about the beauty and value of African culture.

For two years Cobrinha and Moraes tried to persuade João Grande to return to the world of *capoeira*. Finally he agreed to join GCAP and begin teaching at their academy. After his six-year absence he was back as a teacher. Newspaper articles began to appear more frequently, and his fame and influence began to grow. In 1989 he was invited by Mestre Jelon Vieira to tour the United States to discuss and demonstrate *capoeira angola*. Fourteen years earlier Mestre Jelon had first formally introduced *capoeira regional* to the United States.

João Grande's tour was a tremendous success. In California he gave workshops for the school of Mestre Bira Almeida, a writer on *capoeira* and a student of Mestre Bimba. Practitioners of *capoeira regional* were interested in *capoeira angola*. When João Grande returned to Brazil, he was awarded the Brazilian National Sports Medal of Merit by the government. He subsequently received numerous awards and citations. In 1990 he again traveled to the United States to present *capoeira* at the National Black Arts Festival in Atlanta, Georgia. In the same year Mestres João Grande, Moraes, and Cobrinha, and Contra-Mestre Themba Mashama performed at the Schomburg Center for Research in Black Culture in New York City. They were part of an international conference, "Dancing Between Two Worlds: Kongo-Angola Culture and the Americas." Mestre Grande performed *capoeira angola* for then Mayor David Dinkins of New York, and he began teaching an international group of students in that city.

Mestre João Grande, like his teacher Mestre Pastinha, has dedicated his life to the practice and teaching of *capoeira angola*. He too has become a great philosopher of the art. In the newspaper *Portugal/Brazil*, Brazilian artist Claudia Gonçalves has written a beautiful description of João Grande:

> For João Grande, *capoeira* is an exercise of the soul. Its movements inspired by nature [are] so pure that they can be recognized in any and all physical activity. Mestre João identifies these movements in all that he observes: "A person on the bus is able to make a movement of *capoeira*. All that moves, man, child, cat, snake, fish, tree, always make the

movement of *capoeira* . . .

"In *capoeira angola*, premeditated strikes don't exist. All depends on the *capoeirista*. There at the moment can appear techniques never seen before. An *angoleiro* is never able to say that he/she has learned everything about *capoeira*."

This ancient art and its masters teach one how to encounter harsh experiences while remaining flexible and receptive; how to respond to social violence with evasion and grace; and how to use the trials and tribulations of life to develop physical strength, spiritual strength, and wisdom in one's thoughts and actions. *Capoeira angola* is ancestral wisdom passed on so that each person can make the best of their times and possibilities, creating balanced and productive lives, while adding some beauty to the world.

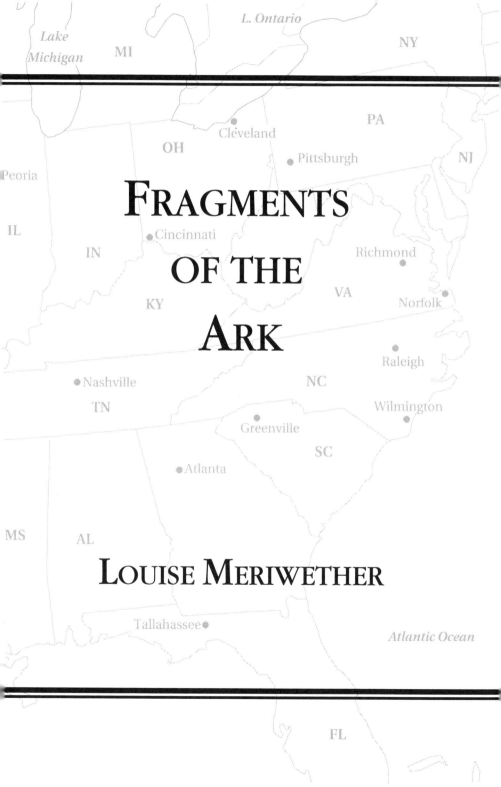

FRAGMENTS

OF THE

ARK

LOUISE MERIWETHER

Louise Meriwether was born in Haverstraw, New York. She holds a bachelor's degree from New York University and a master's degree from the University of California at Los Angeles. She has taught creative writing at Sarah Lawrence College and the University of Houston.

Ms. Meriwether is a free-lance writer and the author of several books, including *Daddy Was a Number Runner* and the children's books *Don't Take the Bus on Monday: The Rosa Parks Story* and *The Freedom Ship of Robert Smalls.* Her short stories have appeared in numerous publications, including *Essence* and *Antioch Review* and in the anthologies *Daughters of Africa* and *Black Women of White America,* among others. Ms. Meriwether has received fiction grants from the New York State Foundation for the Arts, the National Endowment for the Arts, and the Rabinowitz Foundation, among others.

A member of PEN International and a fellow of the Yaddo Artists Colony and the Virginia Center for the Creative Arts, Ms. Meriwether lives in New York City. The following selection is an excerpt from her forthcoming novel *Fragments of the Ark,* to be published in February by Pocket Books.

Charleston, 1856. Peter and Rain met at a funeral held on a Sunday afternoon in order to attract a crowd. Old Esau's funeral. At ninety-two he had been the oldest member of the Brotherhood and Uncle Hiram had promised to put him away in style.

Two white horses were pulling the lorry carrying the pine coffin. Lined up behind it were the Brotherhood men wearing jaunty red scarves to signify their social ties. They were Old Esau's family, his wife was long dead and his children sold away years ago. The musicians were next in line, quietly carrying their instruments, followed by church members, friends, and total strangers. In his coffin the old man was rather cramped but not complaining, wearing a moth-eaten suit he had saved thirty years for his burying.

It was a raggedy procession because folks waiting on the sidelines kept jumping into it. Two women in long rustling skirts were suddenly marching next to Peter, one of them tiny and pretty, wearing a green head wrap.

"Hello," he said, and made himself known. "I is Peter Mango. And what might you name be?"

"Rain."

"So how long you knowed Old Esau?" he asked, making conversation.

"Who?"

"The fellow we is burying."

"Didn't know him at all, but I wants to pay my respects."

It seemed as if the entire colored population of Charleston had come to pay their respects and do Old Esau proud. The pine box fascinated Peter and he stared at it speculatively. Would he be cramped in it? Could he breathe? With a few well-placed holes could a living body hide in it and be driven safely to Philadelphia, maybe? He stole a look at Rain, caught her eye and smiled.

When the procession reached the outskirts of town, the trumpet player raised his horn to his lips. Let the music begin. The drummer came in on the downbeat and then the fiddler. A woman's soprano soared over the treetops.

> . . . Joshua fit the battle of Jericho
> and the walls came tumbling down . . .

They were all singing, the drumbeat lending wings to their feet, banishing weariness. In his coffin Old Esau tapped his foot in time with the music. He had always loved that song, imagining himself to be like Joshua, tumbling down the walls.

At the colored cemetery the weeping willows kneeled to the ground and the few headstones that existed leaned sideways away from the wind. The pine box was laid beside an open grave and the mourners faced Preacher Thomas Large who would deliver the sermon, although it was against the law. In fact, the entire procession was against the law, black people forbidden to congregate in groups of five or more without a white person present. But colored funerals were such protracted affairs that no white minister wanted to be so bothered.

Preacher Large was famous for his spellbinding sermons delivered in praise houses situated deep in the woods which slaves had to sometimes attend surreptitiously. Lanky and dark-skinned, he wore a black sombrero, his pants tucked inside his boots western style like a man used to moving at lightning speed with never a backward glance.

Hiram handed each Brotherhood member a single rose which his fat wife, Helen, had picked earlier. Peter positioned himself next to Rain who was stealing glances at him, at the way he stood flat-footed, his calves curved backward like a scythe. In time she would come to love the way his calves poked out like that against his trousers—and when he pulled them off and his muscular legs pinned her willingly down. But at the moment she was just looking.

The testimonials for Esau began, interspersed with singing. Hiram spoke for the Brotherhood, extolling the virtues of the dear departed. The porters were heard from next, a long eulogy; the old man had once worked with them. A teary woman spoke for the church choir, and on and on the tributes went. Finally, Preacher Large delivered his sermon looking down at the pine box with his fierce, raking eyes which had seen hellfire and the coming of the Lord. He spoke about the trials and tribulations of Esau who, by the time he had hired himself out and saved enough to buy his freedom, was already an old man. But he had not deserted them, just gone ahead to prepare a place for them on high. The preacher chanted.

> I envision God standing on the heights of heaven
> Throwing the devil like a burning torch
> Over the gulf into the valleys of hell,
> His eye the lightning's flash
> His voice the thunder's roll.
> With one hand he snatched the sun from its socket
> And the other he clapped across the moon.
> My God is a mighty God.

The congregation moaned. "Ain't he? Preach, Brother Large."

> Yes, My God is a mighty God
> And we born of the Spirit
> Should cling close to him
> For he has promised to be a shelter
> In the time of storm,
> A rock in a weary land.

"Yes, he is."
"Jesus. Bless thy holy name."

> Our Lord, our deceased brother was born in sin
> And he died in Christ.
> He sold his lot in Egypt
> And he bought a lot in Paradise.
> Ashes to ashes . . .

The Brotherhood flung their roses on top of the coffin. The mourners were in a frenzy, possessed by the spirit, praying they would be liberated from this vale of tears in the sweet by-and-by if not sooner. They stamped their feet, their undulating bodies praising God. Praise His holy name. Hiram's wife threw up her hands, tucked her head under, and executed several fast steps which suspiciously resembled dancing. "I'm gon shout my way to heaven," she cried. "I'm gon sell my lot in Egypt." Tears rolled down her cheeks. Rain was suddenly screaming, a high piercing sound that curdled Peter's blood.

"Mamma," she cried. "Tonk. Alfred. Jamie."

Each name was punctuated by a wail as she flung wide her arms to embrace the invisible. Then she was trembling and would have fallen had Peter not caught her. She sobbed uncontrollably against his chest, so tiny, so stricken, while he dabbed at her tears with his red scarf, touched by her grief.

The procession left the cemetery to the beat of the drums, singing the old songs on their way home, Rain clinging to Peter's hand. They passed a stream and Hiram performed the last ritual. He dropped a white hibiscus into the water and the mourners, knowing its destination, watched it swirl and eddy then right itself and head downstream.

Inside the pine box there was stillness. Old Esau's soul had finally fled. It was curled inside the flower, floating toward the river that emptied into the Atlantic Ocean and would carry him back to the motherland, home to Africa.

Rain was the property of Kenneth Rodman, a banker. Usually on Sundays he allowed her to take the ferry to James Island to visit her daughter and sister on a nursery farm. Peter, acutely smitten, was distressed upon learning the Rain was a mother but naturally anybody so pretty would be taken and he was a donkey's ass for not having realized that.

"Is you baby's daddy here in Charleston?" he asked.

"He ain't in it," Rain replied. "I'm all that Zee's got."

They often met on the ferry come Sunday when they were both returning from James Island. Peter was loaded down with vegetables and fruit toted in a large basket on his head, bought from Sea Island slaves who were allowed to cultivate little plots on their own. He was finding it difficult to court Rain.

"I cain't go out walking with no man," she told him, refusing his request to accompany her home. "You best get them cabbages to your customers 'fore that big basket puts a knot on your head."

In time his persistence prevailed and they did go out walking, Peter falling desperately in love. Kenneth Rodman had brought Rain to Charleston three years ago and made her accompany him to church every Sunday where he was a deacon sitting downstairs and she upstairs in the gallery. Afterward, with the rest of the day off, she scooted over to James Island. Peter kept questioning her about Zee's daddy but Rain was as close-mouthed as she was pretty.

"Why you keep pestering me?" she protested, her burnished eyes flashing, her bottom lip poked out.

"'Cause I is a jealous man."

"Well you ain't got no cause so stop you hounding."

He persisted and she disappeared into a fortress of silence. To coax her out he talked about himself.

"Does you know 'bout the Citadel, Rain? That it was on account of a black man they built it?"

Her eyes widened with surprise. It was a Sunday afternoon and they had been walking. Silently. At Marion Square they paused to look at the massive stone fortress behind it, the Citadel, four stories high with thick impregnable walls and several cannons in the wide courtyard. Peter related the story to Rain as it had been told to him by Uncle Hiram and he also told her about Delia.

It all occurred when he first came to Charleston, a boy of eleven, Mamma left behind in Beaufort. Mamma had persuaded their owner not to sell her child, to let him hire out his time in Charleston. Massa Roland had found him a lamplighting job there and left him with his sister-in-law. Peter finally looked up Mamma's friend, Hiram Jenkins, not so much because of his reluctant promise to do so but because the slaves Peter lived with in a room above the carriage house were so hateful.

First off Stubby, the coachman, informed him, "Massa Pope don't like pickaninnies so I don't know why he letting you live here."

Stubby's ferocious look indicated that the boy's tenure in the slave quarters would be short and miserable, which seemed to be exactly what Delia, the cook, had in mind. The pickaninnies that Cuthbert Pope could not abide had been her children, all four of them, which he had sold as soon as they could toddle. The youngest one, Nooky, Delia had been led to believe she could keep because he had reached the age of ten before she woke up one morning to find him gone. Sold. And his daddy, too. And now they had given her this stump from Beaufort to feed?

It was more than a body could bear, she grumbled, and boxed Peter's ears because he was still a boy but smelled like a man. "Haul that tub out to the yard, Mistuh Stink, and wash yourself." Or she didn't like the corner where he had left his pallet and would kick it elsewhere and then complain. "I is got to fall over you mess every time I come into this room? You is trying to maim me?" She was a short, dumpy woman but her arms were long enough to slap him up beside his head a couple of times a day. The other servants who shared their quarters complained that it had been crowded enough before Peter had been stuck in there.

In exchange for his board he was required to help Stubby keep the stables clean, the horses groomed, and run errands for Loretta Pope. She wasn't as nice as her sister, Peter's mistress in Beaufort, a gentle woman who had never struck him. Missy Loretta had no such sentiments and boxed his ears. She was considered a beauteous southern belle, with smoky gray eyes, a cinched-in waist and the hauteur of a queen. During Charleston's social season she hosted huge parties and pressed Peter into service, dressing him up in red velvet britches. He disliked those evenings intensely, standing at the sideboard motionless until beckoned. When her husband, Cuthbert, complained that she spent money like water, Loretta bitterly reminded him of her station. She had not come to him penniless but with a substantial dowry including a plantation, but he was reducing her to a beggar. He drank heavily and they quarreled often.

Cuthbert Pope did not flog Peter, who was not his property, but used his fists instead. A fist could blacken a boy's eye, bloody his clothes, and scramble his brains so that he fell out from dizziness. Peter fled from home to find Hiram Jenkins. "Tell him," Mamma had said, "that you is Lily Mango's boy."

Peter liked Hiram instantly. He was a heavyset dark-skinned man, his height and breadth commanding but also so comforting that Peter was ready to hold his hand and be led anywhere. It was a trait Hiram had honed, leading people around so effortlessly they barely noticed it. His fleshy face was hairless and so was his head almost, only a few lonesome gray knots growing on it like cactus in a desert.

They became a fixture walking about town, the balding plum-black man and the chubby boy. At the Battery wall staring at the sea-green water, Hiram showed him the spot where the Cooper and Ashley rivers merged. Then they strolled in White Point Gardens admiring the elegant mansions on South Battery.

At Meeting and Broad streets Hiram told him, "This here intersection is the white folks' heart." On each corner were massive colonnaded buildings, their pillars holding up City Hall, the County Courthouse, the Guard House, and St. Michael's Episcopal Church whose bells tolled the hour and warned Negroes at sundown to get their black selves home.

The grandeur of the city impressed Peter, but best of all were the people patting his head and exclaiming, "Lily Mango's boy from Beaufort? Ain't that nice." Said it whether they knew Lily Mango or not, which most of them didn't. Hiram knew them all, the street vendors pulling their carts and singsonging their wares, the Negro craftsmen who owned their little shops, and the colored folks who hawked produce in the stalls on Market Street behind a portico which was a roost for buzzards, the city's scavengers.

But Peter closed his eyes when passing the slave mart, refusing to look at a young girl on the auction block, naked to the waist, being sold to the highest bidder. Or coming across a black man's severed head stuck on a pike outside of town, flies buzzing in his eye sockets and in his blood-caked mouth.

"Open your eyes, boy," Uncle Hiram would growl, walking alongside of him. "How can you remember if you don't see the crap they're throwing in your face? Smell it and eat it, if need be, with your eyes wide open. They may blind you but don't blind yourself." Stubbornly, the boy kept his eyes closed.

Hiram's favorite spot in the city was the Citadel. "They built it on account of a black man thirty some years ago," he told Peter one day and whispered the name as though it might still get him hung. "Denmark Vesey."

"He was a free man by then, bought himself after winning an East Bay lottery. At the time I'm telling you about he owned about eight thousand dollars' worth of property. But his children were all slaves because their mammas were and that riled him. I think he had seven wives and maybe more than one at a time." Uncle Hiram chuckled. "Denmark was a genius, not just with women but in organizing men."

According to witnesses at the trials, about nine thousand slaves from the surrounding countryside had been involved in the insurrection plotted by Denmark Vesey. He justified their right to exterminate their oppressors by quoting from his authority, the Bible. "Behold, the day of the Lord cometh," Hiram quoted, "and thy spoils shall be divided in the midst of thee. For I will gather all nations against Jerusalem to battle, and the city shall be taken and the houses rifled, and the women ravished and half of the city shall go forth into captivity."

Peter was spellbound. "That's in the Bible, Uncle? Those very words?"

"Zechariah, chapter fourteen." Briefly he outlined the insurrectionary plot. Denmark carefully picked for his lieutenants slaves who were so trusted by their masters they had freedom of movement, including three servants of the governor. The slaves were organized into blocks, each with its leader, and commissioned to make bayonets, pike heads, musket balls and to steal powder and combustible fuses from the arsenal. Sites were duly noted where weapons could be obtained at the appointed hour. Each lieutenant was given a specific assignment, and they were to strike simultaneously at several locations, kill every white person they met, and any black who stood in their way. "He that is not with me is against me," Hiram stated. "Luke, chapter eleven, verse twenty-three."

The plan was to take over a ship in the harbor and sail to Haiti where slaves had successfully revolted and were free. Peter's excitement mounted. He was riding with Denmark, a dagger in one hand, a musket in the other, his thighs pressed tightly against his horse.

"The insurrection was betrayed," Hiram said, his face stony, "by a house slave who was invited to join it."

"Betrayed?" Peter repeated, crestfallen.

Betrayal meant the hangman's noose for Denmark Vesey who refused to confess and went to the gallows unrepentant with four of his lieutenants. It meant bloody reprisals throughout the Southland and the arrest of hundreds of slaves. To save themselves—to be banished rather than hung—many pointed a shaky finger at their neighbors. The gallows accepted them, one by one, and stretched their necks into the next world.

"But white folks were still terrified, Peter, ever fearful of having their pale throats slit while they slept. They considered what Denmark had been. A free man. A Bible class leader in the African Methodist Episcopal Church. And a sailor who had traveled with his master, who was a slave trader, to the West Indies and Africa. So they passed laws to hinder all those things, strangling us free Negroes with more restrictions as if we didn't have enough already. The A.M.E. church, built and owned by us, had always been raided, accused of being abolitionist. This time they closed it down entirely and banished our founder. And they jailed all black seamen entering our ports until their boats left. Didn't want them to contaminate us with notions of freedom. That caused an uproar in foreign countries, jailing their folks like that. And finally, Peter, they built that there Citadel, a fortress where white folks could be assembled to protect them from black folks with freedom on their minds."

"Tell me again," Peter begged, "what Denmark Vesey said 'bout slavery."

"That it's an abomination."

"I mean from the Scriptures, 'bout killing we enemies."

"And they utterly destroyed all that was in the city, both man and woman, young and old, and ox and sheep and ass with the edge of the sword."

"You didn't tell me that one before."

"Well I'm telling you now."

"You sure it's in the Bible? Just like that?"

"Joshua, chapter six, verse twenty-one."

"Was you in it, Uncle? Was you one of them riding with—"

Infuriated, Hiram grabbed Peter by his neck and lifted him clean off the ground. "Are you an unreconstructed fool? Don't let your tongue rattle around loose in your head like that."

"I is sorry."

But Peter was certain Uncle Hiram had been among the chosen. And he had to read those Bible passages his own self. That was a certainty also.

In time he did. Uncle Hiram bought him a primer and began teaching him how to read at odd moments, secretly, of course, since it was against the law, an edict constantly bent out of joint. Hiram had been educated in a Negro church school for free children which slave children also ingenuously attended. Supposedly they were delivering laundry or coal or were there on some other pretext, their schoolbooks hidden in their clothing.

Peter, happily obsessed, took to wearing a floppy hat in sunshine and rain, his primer tucked beneath it so he could study at any spare moment. Dodging a backhanded slap from Delia one afternoon, his schoolbook fell to the floor. Pouncing on it like a vulture, she took it to her mistress. Outraged, Loretta Pope beat Peter over the head with a stick until his nose bled.

When Peter's master visited Charleston he was apprised of the boy's sins and angrily threatened to sell him. Peter was duly frightened. Sell him? At one of the slave auctions held every week at Ryan's jail? He was to be chained in a coffle, marched to Georgia and disappear forever? Never to see Mamma again? Or Uncle Hiram and his friends? Terrified, he dug a hole under the pecan tree next to the carriage house and buried his primer.

Delia's turn came next. She burned the roast for a party, insisted it was an accident, but Cuthbert Pope roared that she had been insolent in front of his guests and he intended to whip all the sass out of her. So saying he tied her hands to a beam in the stable and flogged her with his whip until she was bloody. Peter was a horrified witness as was Missy Loretta, who attempted to stop her husband after the first few lashes and Delia screaming, "Mercy, massa. Oh God. Somebody. Have mercy."

"That's enough, Cuthbert. Cut her down." Loretta didn't think highly of colored people but there were exceptions and Delia was one of them.

But Cuthbert Pope seemed possessed with the whipping, his face crimson with anger. "Bloody bitch," he shouted and Peter didn't know whether he was cursing poor Delia or Missy who was struggling with him, trying to grab hold of the whip.

"You want to kill her?" she cried. "Stop it."

Violently Cuthbert flung his wife away from him, sending her crashing into the wall.

"It's me you really want to whip," she screamed and ran crying from the stable.

He whipped Delia until a bone protruded from her bloody back and he was exhausted. She was unconscious when Stubby and another servant cut her down, and Peter helped them carry her to the carriage house. He ran to fetch water in an earthen jug and watched Stubby attempting to staunch the flow of blood, tears in the old man's eyes. They took turns sitting by Delia's pallet all night, trying to keep her fevered brow cool with some evil-smelling herbs in a gunnysack.

It was around midnight when she came to herself and stared at the shadow squatting beside her. "Boy," she whispered. "That you?" She never called Peter anything but boy. "Is that you, Nooky?"

Peter thought a lie might comfort her. "Yes, ma'am."

But Delia, though pain-ridden and delirious, knew her own child from an impostor. With the strength of a madman she rose up and screamed, "Liar," and hurled the water jug at his head. He ducked and it cracked open on the floor.

Weeks later, when she was somewhat recovered, Peter moved out of their room to a corner of the stable. He found the horses preferable to Delia.

"She's a bitter pill," Uncle Hiram said. "Poor thing. She never got over her husband being sold, too, after all of their children. He was a man that could gentle her down." She was a woman, Peter felt, who needed plenty of gentling.

Then came the day they took Delia away, threw her into an isolated hole in the workhouse to await her trial. It was brief, the charges read and the prisoner found guilty of attempted murder, of feeding her master daily a minute quantity of poison in his turtle soup, his chicken broth, his lamb stew. Cuthbert Pope did not die from Delia's ministrations only because she used a touch too much one evening, perhaps her hands shook, and his stomach rebelled. A doctor hastily called—who had been involved in a similar case—uncovered the foul play.

Peter stood outside the workhouse the day the verdict was rendered. The judge ruled Delia was to be hung promptly and without fanfare. There would be no glaring headlines to nourish another trusted cook into becoming a would-be assassin.

Delia emerged from the workhouse in chains between two guards, half carried, half dragged to a coach for her trip to the gallows two miles outside of Charleston. She stumbled, almost fell, and as she was hauled to her feet she saw Peter.

"Boy," she mumbled.

"Yes, ma'am."

"Peter?" It was the first time she had ever called him by his name. "Peter," she repeated more firmly and nodded to herself. Her eyes were not glazed, not crazy, but her lips had parted to curl at the corners.

Was it a frown, Peter wondered? Were her chains too tight? Or had Delia smiled at him?

The next day he dug up his speller from under the pecan tree.

"Poor Delia," Rain groaned, when Peter told her about the cook. "It's so hard for a mother to lose her chile."

Peter said, "It be hard for a father, too. Maybe your daughter's daddy misses—"

"No," Rain interrupted, agitated. "He . . . he don't know her." Peter appeared puzzled and she explained. "He went away."

"With his master?"

She nodded.

"Did you love him?"

"No," Rain whispered sadly.

On those Sunday afternoons not spent with Rain, and after delivering his produce, Peter attended meetings of the benevolent society founded by Hiram, the Brotherhood for Justice and Equality for People of African Descent. He paid his dues which went into a burial and pension fund and listened to the articles Hiram read aloud which could get them all jailed. Periodically Negro seamen from the North smuggled abolitionist pamphlets to Hiram, bypassing the postmaster's zeal for consigning such seditious material to his regular bonfires. Consigned to flames as well were the homes of "nigger lovers," critics of slavery, sometimes with the critic inside being charred to a crisp. This naturally created a steady exodus of liberal white folks to safer ground.

This Sunday afternoon the meeting was well under way in the storage room of Trinity Methodist Church when Peter arrived. The room was filled with old files, dusty boxes, and spiders spinning cobwebs in the corners. Hiram sat at a rickety table amid the clutter, a kerosene lamp at his elbow, and a large open Bible in front of him. The Bible was his shield. Beads of perspiration danced on his balding head, the room was hot and windowless. A dozen or so Brotherhood members faced him perched on stools.

Peter eased into a seat next to Gimpy, the glazier. The men were discussing the financial problems of Widow Johnson and her five children. The little pension she received from the Brotherhood—her husband had been a member—was proving woefully inadequate. Samuel, the ironworker, offered to hire her oldest boy in response to Hiram's request for help.

"Good. I'm sure Widow Johnson will be most grateful." Hiram leaned over the table, blessing Samuel with a warm smile of appreciation, his head slightly tilted to one side, a habit of his, especially when he was listening to someone's troubles, completely absorbed. He opened the table drawer that was lined with a cardboard picture of Jesus Christ and extracting from under it a newspaper, waved it in the air.

"Here's a little something which swam down to us from Boston."

The Brothers chuckled. Peter sat up straighter. He hoped it was his favorite, the *North Star*, written by Frederick Douglass, a runaway slave who was now a fiery abolitionist. Or Lloyd Garrison's paper, *The Liberator*. That man hated slavery so fiercely it was sometimes hard to remember he wasn't a darky.

"You all remember that article that was in the *Mercury* a few weeks back?" Uncle Hiram asked. "About an abolitionist name of John Brown? I read it to you."

The Brothers did indeed remember. The *Charleston Mercury* had called John Brown the scum of the earth, castigating him and his band of cutthroats for murdering five settlers in cold blood on the banks of the Pottawatomie River in Kansas.

Peter understood that the bloodletting in Kansas was about land. And about them. Colored folks. Slaves. Uncle Hiram had spelled it out fully at earlier meetings. It was a question of economics and political power. For nearly forty years whenever a new state applied to join the Union the North and South quarreled ferociously, South Carolina constantly threatening to secede and drag the rest of the South along with her. They demanded that the new states be slave while the North demanded that they be free. Congress always pried the belligerents apart with compromises but blood was spilled in Kansas. Both the Pro-Slavers and Free Soilers rushed settlers into the area to decide the matter by vote and in the process raid farms, stuff ballot boxes, and shoot each other's brains out. But being against slavery in the territory did not mean Free Soilers necessarily welcomed competition with freedmen. Most of them wanted the land for white men only.

"This article sheds more light on John Brown's raid than the *Mercury* reported," Uncle Hiram said.

"Uh huh," the Brothers grunted, suspicious of whatever the *Charleston Mercury* printed. The newspaper was edited by one of the Rhetts, a powerful slaveholding family that for years had advocated secession.

Hiram quickly read the piece which reported that a band of Pro-Slavers on horseback had ridden into Lawrence, a

Free Soil settlement, and sacked it, killing the livestock and burning the place to the ground. In retaliation, John Brown and his followers rode to the Pottawatomie and killed five of the marauders. Brown, a fervent abolitionist and former Underground Railroad conductor, declared that he was an instrument of God.

Peter felt a thrill of excitement. The killings were terrible but also grand. *Behold, the day of the Lord cometh . . . and the city shall be taken and the houses rifled, and the women ravished . . .*

As if reading his mind, Gimpy, the glazier, shook his head, his double chins trembling. "Vengeance is mine sayeth the Lord," he intoned solemnly.

Hiram suddenly stiffened, his head cocked toward the door and the Brothers also became a listening post. A floorboard had creaked outside the storage room, a deliberately weakened floorboard. Footsteps were approaching. Hiram opened the table drawer and slipped the newspaper under the cardboard picture of Jesus Christ, a sanctuary for the seditious.

Their minister, Reverend Damon, stuck his head through the door followed by his pot belly, his presence legitimizing the meeting. He was a huge man with a booming voice to cast out devils and make his flock tremble in fear at the wrath of God. And he was also Hiram's guardian—a requirement for every free Negro—and had bailed him out of jail more than once for conducting his illegal meetings at his house.

After the A.M.E. Church had been shut down following the Denmark Vesey affair, the benevolent societies which had used its facilities went underground and for years their meetings were raided and their leaders jailed. Reverend Damon was among those who protested that it was ridiculous to forbid blacks to meet to pool their money and bury their dead. Since they intended to congregate anyway despite laws to the contrary, common sense dictated that their meetings should be conducted openly under watchful eyes. He joined those pressuring the Methodists to allow Negroes to have a separate church again, but this time under a white minister, himself, instead of a colored rabble-rouser who might preach insurrection.

"Am I interrupting your meeting?" he asked.

"We were just about to finish with a reading from the Bible, suh." Hiram glanced down, read several lines from First Corinthians, chapter one, then closed the good book with a flourish.

"Amen," Peter intoned along with the Brothers, nodding his head piously.

He noticed how sweetly Reverend Damon smiled at Uncle Hiram, their Bible class leader. The two were fond of each other within the boundaries allowed, one man duty-bound to vigilance, the other man duty-bound to subvert it. Having done his duty by putting in an appearance, Reverend Damon led the Brothers upstairs into the light.

Left behind in the table drawer, Jesus Christ finished reading the Boston newspaper.

Peter learned nothing more about Rain's past until the Sunday she failed to appear on the ferry. After delivering his produce he went to find her, rapping on the back door of her owner's brick house on Broad Street.

A haggard Rain opened the door, her face caved in on itself, her eyes puffy from crying. Her thick hair was standing up on end as though she had been trying to pull it out at the roots. She flung herself forward and darted past Peter, a tiny wild woman running she knew not where. He caught Rain before she reached the wrought-iron gate and she fell against him sobbing.

"They is gone and I is got to find them."

She strained against Peter, trying to escape from the band of his arms but he held her fast.

"Rain, what's wrong?"

It took a while for her sobs to subside, for the words to come in snatches. This morning after church as she had prepared to leave for the ferry Massa Rodman had told her the news.

"He didn't know Massa Slater were gon do it. That they—"

"Who he?" Peter interrupted. "Who's Massa Slater?"

"He own my Zee and Petunia. He put them on that nursery farm." Rain looked at Peter piteously and asked, "How this happen? Not again. Why, Lord? Why?"

"Rain. Please. Tell me what . . ."

"My baby and li'l sister's gone. Sold to a slave trader. Gone to Georgia."

Peter's heart flipped over and the earth stood still. The birds forgot to sing and the wind refused to whistle. The only sound was Rain moaning.

"My babies is gone. Gone."

She was crying again and he didn't know what to do. Choke her to stop that infernal wailing which was hammering nails into his flesh? But there was no place to run to, no place to hide.

"Gone," Rain shrieked again.

Her heartbreak resounded down the long tunnel of Peter's years and found him lacking. He reached out to hold her, feeling useless, but Rain pushed him away.

"I has to go 'fore Massa comes looking for me."

Peter watched her trudge inside. Motionless, he stood straddle-legged, his misery unbearable because there was nothing that a grown man, a black man, a slave could do. Except kill somebody.

*   *   *

In the weeks that followed, Peter glued the story together, the little pieces that Rain reluctantly revealed, rooted as they were in pain. She had lived with her mother, Elizabeth, and her five brothers on a plantation near the Combahee River. After her child and sister were born, Rain's family was sold, scattered like seeds in the wind. She didn't know where any of them were, except for the babies placed on the nursery farm.

"Every time I went there they cried when I left," Rain mourned. "My poor darlings. God, where is they?"

It took months for her to recover. Peter held her in his arms when she was forlorn and when she was demented.

Rain told him once, "I loves you 'cause you is strong but gentle." She whispered it shyly, a slave woman not accustomed to gentleness.

The following year, in the autumn when the leaves were the burnished color of Rain's eyes, their owners gave them permission to marry.

Glory was born the year they hung John Brown and Peter went berserk.

Brown had attacked the federal arsenal at Harpers Ferry to obtain ammunition for a slave uprising. Despite the shadow of the noose, his unrepentant defense that slavery was an immoral act offensive to God swayed many who had never been swayed before into supporting abolition. Brown's hanging, along with two of the black men who had ridden with him, depressed Peter who had been feeling a nudge of lunacy ever since his daughter's birth. Twice he had approached Rain's owner offering to buy Glory's freedom and had been abruptly dismissed.

Finally Peter's nudge became a shove one moonless night and he raced to Kenneth Rodman's house babbling like a madman that he would kill his child if Massa didn't sell her and Rain to him. Kill his daughter because she had no rights. That's what the judge had said denying poor

Dred Scott his freedom.

"My Glory ain't got no rights," Peter yelled, bruised anew. "Any white man can beat my chile. Rape her. Kill her." Peter's bushy hair was standing on end, his eyes gone mad in their sockets.

Kenneth Rodman, startled out of his sleep by this nigra banging on his door before dawn, fumed, "I've never beaten Rain nor intend to rape her child." Stringy and asthmatic, he blew his nose, honking like a goose.

"I'll kill them both," Peter raved, adding Rain to his list of victims. "And didn't Isaiah say in the Bible, is such a fast I have chosen to loose the bands of wickedness, to undo the heavy burdens, to let the oppressed go free and break every yoke."

The white man blinked, looking quite fragile with his thin silver hair framing his gaunt face. "Don't lecture me, you black ape. I've searched my soul and find it free of guilt."

They were standing in the foyer, Kenneth Rodman in his nightdress, having been summoned to the door by a frightened servant.

"But you ain't search my soul," Peter lamented. "And I ain't gon let it kill me slowly watching my baby grow up a slave. If you don't let me buy—"

"Stop threatening me. Do you honestly believe you can frighten me? A deacon in the church and a man of God? I've done nothing to Rain except try to instill a sense of virtue in her so she wouldn't turn into a slut like her mother."

Peter was surprised, knowing nothing about the supposed sluttishness of his wife's mother. "Rain ain't no slut."

"At least I've been successful in that regard."

Peter felt his madness slipping into despair. God, help me, he prayed. Massa Rodman was looking at him warily and their eyes met, interlocking as though connected by an axle that had dragged them from birth to this decisive moment.

"Before God," Peter ranted, "I'll—"

Rodman interrupted, his voice wheezy, "Everybody calls upon God to be their witness." He started to cough, choking, his face flushed. He tried to speak but was unable to and beckoned for Peter to accompany him.

Peter followed him down a carpeted hall to a room where a fire was already burning in the grate. Kenneth Rodman staggered to his desk, sat down, and stopped choking. He regarded Peter with resentment and finally sighed.

"You're a Christian," he said, "and persistent. That's in your favor. I have discovered that persistence usually pays off."

It certainly had paid off for him, a wealthy man by dint of three plantations he had gained by foreclosing on their owners. He started to cough again, picked up a pen and his seizure ceased. Shaking his head and muttering to himself about the mysterious ways of God, Kenneth Rodman slowly wrote a note on a scrap of paper and handed it to Peter.

"Now get out of my house," he ordered, "before I change my mind."

Rain greeted Peter with relief when he arrived at home, aware that he had been acting peculiar.

"Honeybunch, listen." Slowly he read the note to her, stumbling over the words. "Being of sound mind and body I hereby agree to free my slaves Rain and Glory Mango upon receipt of eight hundred dollars. Kenneth Rodman."

"For me?" Rain asked, her eyes wide with disbelief, her bottom lip quivering.

Peter nodded, almost too filled with joy to speak.

"For me and our baby? Oh, Sugarfoot." Tears were streaming down her face.

"Massa Rodman said you ain't no slut like you mother." Peter wiped a teardrop off Rain's cheek with a forefinger.

"My mamma a slut?" She shook her head. "Massa Rodman didn't know her. All she wanted was for her children be free. Like I is gon be, Peter? Me and Glory?"

"Yes," he whispered and kissed her.

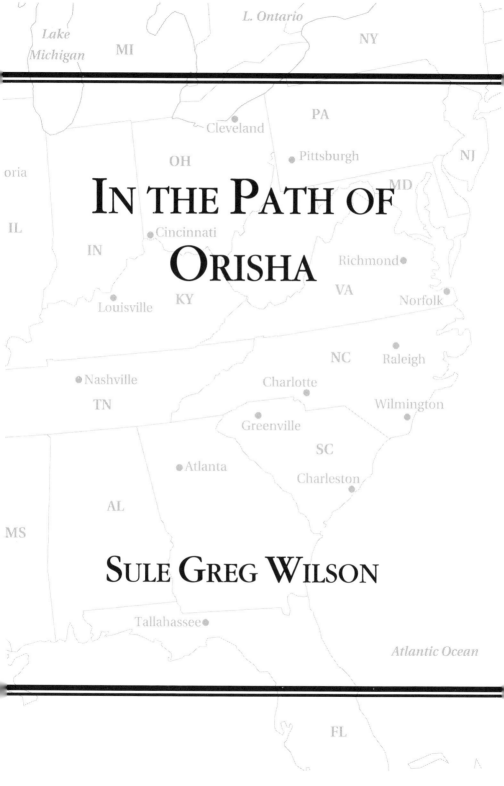

IN THE PATH OF
ORISHA

SULE GREG WILSON

Sule Greg Wilson was born in Washington, DC. He received a BFA and an MA from New York University.

Mr. Wilson has worked as an archivist and archives consultant at the Smithsonian Institution, the Schomburg Center for Research in Black Culture of the New York Public Library, and the World Bank, among others. He has taught and lectured extensively on African and African Diaspora history, culture, spirituality, and traditional theater. He has produced and directed videos, including works for Oracle of Tehuti Video, the Harlem Renaissance Dance Company, and New York University. In addition he has recorded four albums of African music.

Mr. Wilson's work has appeared in *Tantra: The Magazine*, the *Washington Post*, the *Village Voice*, and the *Schomburg Center Journal*, among others. He is the author of *The Drummer's Path: Moving the Spirit with Ritual and Traditional Drumming*. The following selection is adapted from his forthcoming book, *Forms of the Spirit*, to be published in 1995 by Inner Traditions.

Mr. Wilson is a project specialist in the African American Index Project at the Museum of American History, Smithsonian Institution. He lives in Takoma Park, Maryland, with his wife, Vanessa Thomas-Wilson, and their two children.

I was born in 1957 at Freedman's Hospital in Washington, DC, on the campus of Howard University, part of a long tradition of association with that school. My great-grandfather, James Monroe Gregory, was in Howard's first graduating class, having transferred from Oberlin College in 1868 to the new institution established expressly for colored, both African and native. James's son, T. Montgomery Gregory, my grandfather, grew up on campus and returned to the University to teach English and drama. Ernest J. Wilson, my daddy, left Philadelphia to attend Howard. In 1947 he married Montgomery Gregory's fifth child and second daughter, Mignon, my mommy.

Mignon and Ernie didn't meet on campus, though. After the era of the New Negro* was over, my mother's family moved to Atlantic City, New Jersey, "America's Playground." T. Monty, "Pop-pop," was principal of the New Jersey Avenue School, the city's colored high school. Mommy was the baby sister of my daddy's runnin' buddy Hugh Gregory, a Tuskegee airman who, like my daddy, was raising tuition money in that first postwar summer of '46 by waiting tables at resort hotels on the Boardwalk. Mignon Gregory and Ernest Wilson hit it off, and eventually they made three, including me: Gregory C. Wilson, part of each.

My father, like his father-in-law, was "into Africa," and that sense of heritage and pride was infused into me and my big brother and sister. My world has always included Kongo masks, Yoruba country cloth, Bambara sculptures, and plenty books. In my own home today, next to the saber he carried as an officer of colored troops in World War I, is the

*Era of the New Negro—also known as the Harlem Renaissance. A period from World War I into the Great Depression during which the second generation of African-Americans born out of slavery were able to capitalize on education and talent to move the race forward.

African spear (is it Maasai, or a Zulu assagai?) that Pop-pop used as a stage prop for the Howard Players.

My family's conversation arena was the kitchen table, where bread was broken and tradition passed on. Sometimes, Daddy would prop his elbows on the tomato-red formica and pontificate on "ancestor worship." Immediately my sister Wendy would snap to correct him: "It's not *worship!* It's reverence and prayers to the ancestors to speak to God on behalf of the living! You wouldn't go straight to the company president; you'd talk with your boss first. It's respect, Dah-deee! They don't *worship* them!"

Despite all that, none of us made the connection between that down-home intellectual repartee and the ritual of going to my grandparents' house and poring over photo albums and old paintings and postcards; of having family stories told again and again over those photos or over dinner or holiday feasts; of hearing the story of Great-great-great-grandfather Mahammitt sailing from Madagascar ("The Land of the Ancestors") to Maryland, and purchasing Jane, a slave child of Supreme Court Chief Justice Roger B. Taney, to be his wife; of Daddy visiting his Choctaw Grandma Mutt on the reservation; or of the family ritual of approaching the Christmas tree only after parents had arisen and coming downstairs in line, eldest to youngest. "Ancestor worship?" Naaah!

Growing up, I was exposed to other worlds: Africa, Asia, the West Indies. Through that, I learned to see ritual and not be afraid: I'd sat in the audience for ceremonies staged at Howard University's International Night, or by guest dance companies from around the world. I'd witnessed real rituals at Grandma Charlie's Apostolic church in Philadelphia, where elders washed the congregation's feet; I just stared and stared. In 1970 I took part in my big brother's African wedding, performed by the Chief Priest of the Akans of America, Nana Yao Opare Dinizulu. By that time I was two years into African drumming and dancing, and besides, I was a member of the wedding party. All my life I'd seen Spirit at work and been told of visitations and haints and Grandma Charlie's clothes all gone—closets empty!—after she died. From taking all this in, I had an urgent need to synthesize my experiences. I needed perspective, a cosmology. When I was little I wanted to be a paleontologist; you know, a fossil scientist. That's one way to know the ancient world. But in junior high I learned a new way: dancing and drumming, communing with the ways of the ancestors, discerning my creative force—not only Shango, the arrogant cigar-smoking patron of the drums, but also, through attention and breath and dance and having to support the music when others fell behind, with the yin side, Olokun, the Deep Waters.

Things kind of came to a head away from home. I was a sophomore at Oberlin College in Ohio (the same one my great-grands attended—hand of the ancestors?), and I knew I had to get out of Dodge—I sure wasn't getting anywhere in a dry town on the plains thirty-five miles southwest of Cleveland, allegedly an earth sciences major. Some scientist! I spent most of my time in the Conservatory, practicing marimba or trap set or tabla drums. When you tell your geology professor that the limestone in the road cut you're examining for trilobite fossils has exquisite texture for lithography, and he looks at you like you just said, "Who needs pure science? Let's go work for Exxon!"—it's a sign: Time to go.

To accomplish all that I wanted, needed—to dig deep into my spirituality, and find its cultural roots—I had to leave Oberlin. For me, there were two choices: Africa, or New York City. I knew no one in Africa. I had family in New York. And I had to finish school, so New York it was. Somehow, hand of God, I believe, or ancestors whispering in my ear, I was dead-to-rights certain that the only way I could be the person I wanted to become was to become

59

him in that city.

I'd already tasted the Apple. With a friend, I had explored the Village and scoured midtown in search of rhinestones and adventure. In our decorated jeans, we had crashed Sly Stone's wedding reception and talked with the not-all-with-it Mitch Mitchell, Jimi Hendrix's drummer. I had scouted the city three times en route from DC to Ohio. I was ready!

When I arrived in New York June 1, 1977, I already knew how to drum. Since junior high they'd said I was good. Proof had come the year before when for my winter term project I had studied at Babatunde Olantunji's Center for African Culture in Harlem. In less than a fortnight there I was on stage, playing conga drum, songba drum, *and* bell, with the legendary Baba before me and Kehinde Stewart, a bad djembe player, to my right. Now, back in New York, I needed to learn *what* to play, and *when* to play it.

On June 14 I set out to meet Neil Clarke, one of the musicians with the International Afrikan American Ballet. This "supergroup," composed of dancers and drummers who had known each other for years, had studied movement, music, religion, and culture with masters from Ghana, Nigeria, Zaire, Guinea, Cuba, Mali, and Senegal. The year before I transferred to NYU, they had formed their own ensemble, independent of any African-born leader, and they gave their first concert that December. Everyone I asked told me they were the ones who had what I was looking for.

So, on that night in June I left my cousin's place in Manhattan and took, for the first time, the two-subways-and-bus trip that was to become a weekly ritual for the next two years. Djembe and songba drumbeats blasted in the humid storefront space of the New Horizons Center in St. Albans, Queens. I asked for Neil, and when the light-skinned guy playing djembe drum was pointed out to me, I said, "Oh no!" I had seen that drummer before.

Last summer, home from school, my drum-making teacher, Baile, told me I should experience Philadelphia's Ile Ife Day celebration. I rode up with DC's African Heritage Dancers and Drummers. We pulled up in the middle of a parade—masquerades, vendors, drumming, and dancing! What a scene! They didn't do *this* back home!

Wandering around from wonder to wonder, I gravitated to a small park, and the jammin'est drums of a day full of jammin' drums. I worked my way through the sweaty, four-deep circle of people around the musicians; I wanted to see who these folks was! I poked my head in, and my mouth fell open. Here was this one light-skinned guy with red hair and freckles, a bright blue African-style shirt, and fat fingers, playing three congas at once and doing it well enough to have drawn this big a crowd! Folks were congregated around that energy like bees at a soda can, noddin' and groovin' and swayin' and clappin', beating on cans, bottles, and benches, keeping time and laughing and smiling and singing. I couldn't believe what I saw. To this day, sixteen years later, I hold that image clear. And *this* was the man I was told to search for. I found him and there he was, gettin' down even harder than before with a bunch of people at least as good as he was. Now I could see just how hard I had to work. This was New York.

The work was more than just drumming. I was involved in that group's world from 1977 to 1982, with my eyes open; dancing, drumming, singing, and becoming ritualized. As craftspeople, we fashioned instruments and costumes in line with tradition and with sober intent: mirrors flash away negativity, triangles empower, movement engages. As ceremonial musicians, we played at Yoruba diaspora rituals called *bembes*. We were blessed to play before and with elders from here and abroad.

The company's slogan read: "We do magical work, in a magical way. We give magical service, for magical pay."

Purveyors of good vibes and dedicated folklorists, we did our stage shows, sometimes two and three in a day, at venues as varied as Sing Sing prison upstate, and Lincoln Center on Broadway. And before every program, we formed a circle and prayed that we pass love and ancestral power to those who came to see us. Masquerades were danced not as a costume show, but as ritual, with prayers, libations, humility, and faith; folks beyond the footlights just don't know.

This was a traditional, ritual world. The effects of drum and ceremony entered me in different ways. As photographer for International Afrikan American Ballet (I shot for them first; after a year I danced and played on stage), I had to attune myself to the intensity of energy put out by the dancers, drummers, and singers. Then my photography flowed with the show, using its energy to zoom me up and down aisles and between spectators, extending or contracting my body into precise position moments before the performers reached their crescendo. It was fun, and an experience of learning, of acculturating. And sometimes I'd get that tingly, time-shift feeling; I'd look around and that show on stage would shift from choreography to reality as, in the middle of one of her feet-this-way, arms-that-way, head-back-and-forth steps, Amina's eyes would unfocus and roll, and she'd shimmer, stagger back as Spirit entered, and Fatima and Mabel would step out the chorus and whisk the God-touched woman offstage.

People in "The Culture" got to know me through my work and shared with me history and tradition, talk of music and spirit and what it can do. Soon life forced a decision: camera bag, or drum bag?

I played in the parks—Central, Prospect, Washington Square; I played drums in Queens, at City College in Manhattan, at the Restoration in Bed-Stuy, Brooklyn. Playing with others for hours, I became more sensitve to change of the energy: With a whisk of power, making music could be a breeze, or an uphill climb. Observing, I learned who of the New York drum/cultural community walked with Power, with *ashé*. I watched, to discover: How did they carry themselves, how did they wield their power?

I learned that in the traditional world the use of power is conditional, sanctioned. It always manifests in forms; culture gives the keys we are taught to recognize: color, clothing, design, word, gesture. When Amina flew offstage in possession, it was accepted, understood, though a little embarrassing. She was an initiate, had beads and incised scars. My own trance experiences had no sanction, no formal explanation, no society. I kept them to myself.

As a part of tradition, and to insure harmony, a traditional priest was consulted by International, a spiritual reading was done, and it was determined that we had to perform an annual service for the Orisha, the vehicles of God as defined in the Yoruba religion. Though not initiated into that religion, I helped construct altars, ritually clean the space, sing, dance, and play music. I saw power drawn from blood and leaves, from alcohol and smoke. I learned of the Guerreros* kept by the door, experienced the use of chickens, cigars, and corn. I watched, felt, and made the effect of song and spinning, spinning dance. The time was of drums, rum, and good meals of plantains, avocado, and peas-and-rice to keep us strong and playing. They usually had chicken, too, but I'm vegetarian.

And, when the deities came, they came! You could feel it! The air shimmered, sound sparkled, everything went into hyperspace. Perhaps from the rear you'd hear the cry of Spirit entering someone's body. Perhaps up front, a master dancer's eyes would roll, body shuddering, steps flying. And when God took hold, the dancer would dive

---

*Guerreros—this refers both to the collective altars for protective warrior energy and to three of the deities themselves—Ochosi, Ogun, and Elegba.

into the drums. Best to keep your eyes open.

If certain personalities, powerful carriers of the Gods, walked in, the whole place would buzz; now you knew the service was gonna have to rock. I remember Pepe, who carried a wild Elegba (Orisha of the Road, Controller of the Gates, one of the Guerreros), calling out "'Bau! 'Bau! 'Bau!" and smearing palm oil on everyone who God told him needed the blessing of the Opener of the Way. Gettin' on the Good Foot with a red-and-black stick crooked 'round his neck, he'd grab a partner and enjoin everyone in the place to dance. It would rock, it would sway. Folks'd be giggling—Elegba loves laughter and trickery—candy and tobacco would fly, and eventually some people would be told off about some stuff they thought they were doing behind closed doors. You see, Elegba lurks in corners, waiting to show you your own folly and impress upon you the constant need for humility before God, who is everywhere and everything.

Perhaps Shango (the Man's Man, the Lover, the King) would come and, laughing mightily, bless the drums (or berate the drummers if they weren't giving the music all they had). Oshun (Orisha of sweet water, and sweetness) would smear honey across your face, reminding you of the power of sex and sensuality. Or Ogun (Guerrero/warrior of iron, the Untamed Man) would fly in, and all eyes would stay on that machete. Through all this, one learned respect, propriety. I took it all in, tasted the bitter herbs, inhaled the acrid smoke, licked the sweetness, took in the spray of empowered rum like holy water flicked upon the crowd.

Those experiences awakened me. Though not an initiate, not "made" in that religion, I felt and knew when the deities were coming, felt the Power sweeping down through me and all present, peering into souls, inspecting for whom to take. It made my eyes wide, it made my head light, it made me nervous. Sometimes I was almost gone.

Even so, protocol demanded that only those initiated could take that power in and manifest it before all.

Being a "horse" for the God was not my place. I was not *Iyawo*, an initiate wearing only white for one whole year, consecrated for life to embody a specific energy frequency through sacrifice, diet, meditation, and taboo. My head was not "opened." I didn't know the secret signs, I didn't know the sacred songs. Yet, I knew when it was deity time. I knew when God came down to claim a body. That counted for something, didn't it? And I knew, though I had not yet done it alone, that I could call the Gods down with Spirit and energy through music and song to visit the people and hold forth the righteous ways. But, I had no *ocha* (designated deity), no *eleke* (ceremonial necklace that helps focus energy). I had not sat in state in one corner of one room for a week, head shaved, herbed and canopied, and been ritualized and empowered with the blood of plants and animals and the words of man. Despite that, I knew when God was there and was about to take someone down, and out. What did that make me, an outsider who had not been doused, and blessed, and sanctified, and required to pay thousands of dollars to receive the Power? What was it that made me aware, without all that? Did I really need the initiation? What would I be with it?

I went to a *bembe* given by Otello, one of the few Babalaos, or Yoruba diaspora high priests, in New York who initiated US Africans into a spiritual "house." The International drummers were asked to play for his Obatalá *ocha* party.

It was an early spring Sunday, with enough solar momentum to warm not just faces, but the air and the pavement as well. Silken air, fresh from caressing new spring growth, circled my bare forearms as I neared the given address. From the outside, you wouldn't know an African ceremony was about to take place; cars were double-parked, people in white lounged around. Perhaps it's first communion for a little Latina in pastel ribbons, lace gloves, and multiple petticoats. Perhaps it's a wedding reception. Perhaps. I said "hello" to the slim young guy standing by the steps to the basement, and entered the sacred space.

Inside there was lace, and ribbons hung from the door jamb, and a festive atmosphere. Fresh fruit, bananas and such, hung from the rafters. I could immediately smell food being prepared. Beans and rice, plantains and . . . stewed chicken. With pepper. There was energy there. Expectancy, and purpose, and . . . The Elegba shrine by the door was small, makeshift-looking. The conical mud figure with cowrie-shell eyes had a cigar to his white cowrie mouth. He seemed to smile. I went on in.

Children, parents, older women—with gingham aprons protecting their bright white dresses—bustled in and out of the kitchen on the right. Empty chairs lined the left wall. I saw no one that I knew. The basement turned, L-shaped . . . I stopped. Look at that shrine! Coils and coils of white beads poured from the bone china tureen, boiled white yams and coconut galore hid the plates beneath them, white brocade and damask and satin layered the shrine nearly to the ceiling. White votive and seven-day candles blazed. Beautiful white roses in crystal vases graced each tier of the altar. More cloth, suspended from crossbeams over the shrine, formed a soft white sanctuary canopy. I felt the reverence; I bent my knee as I passed.

The musicians' space was opposite the shrine. I took a seat against the wall and waited for those I knew to appear.

Soon the low basement starts getting crowded. More and more folks come, most in white, most older than me. Thick Spanish flies by, peppered with a little English. People in multicolored bead necklaces—red-and-white for Shango, blue-and-white for Yemaya, and orange, deep blue—greet in the right-shoulders-touch, left-shoulders-touch ritual form, laugh and slap backs. Some smoke. It's getting hot in here! I move back across to the kitchen, get a ginger ale in a paper cup, and lean in the shadow against the cool basement wall and sip. Still, no friends.

There's commotion by the door; people are shuffling to make way in the narrow entrance. I hear a familiar laugh, the trademark wild one of my child-of-Elegba buddy/teacher Martin, then the crack-leather sound of him giving somebody five so hard! as he always does. I breathe fully, again. The drummers are here.

As they unpack their instruments—two conga, *shekere*, and bell—I make my way back to the far end of the basement. Because this ceremony is in thanks for the life gifts that Obatalá, the Orisha of purity and patience, has given to the chief priest putting on the *bembe*, the mood is "cool"; not much joking or ribaldry. Folks are relatively subdued, though the fervor of spring eases in each time a person squeezes in from the outside. The host appears: a big guy with white hair, broad across the body like my uncles; he speaks to the musicians. In a white "panama"-style shirt, he's relaxed; it's his house, his show.

I softly greet my teachers, Red, Phil, and Martin, and Amina, Red's wife, who's here to lead the congregation in song. Drums are tuned, the musicians settle in; it is time to begin. I stand behind the drummers where I can watch the whole room, yet give aid, if asked. Red's cigarette-chiseled voice: "Here! Play the bell!" Okay . . . I swallow, slow my breath, settle the instrument in my fingers and look again at my fellows. Amina would start us off. Let's go.

"I-bara go, Ago Mojubara! I—" Boom! and the music starts in on her second syllable. This makes my spirit belong. It's so tight, so purposeful, so alive, so intense; it's real. I tune in my awareness and cool down, make sure my music is way down in the mix, and settle into the groove. "Chink! Chink, k-ching-ching, Chink! K-chink! Chink, k-ching-ching, Chink!" goes the bell, and I hold the rhythm right there, no matter who's singing what, who's playing what, who's dancing what. All afternoon: in Elegba's chant, and on through the litany. With fat cigars, lucky leaves, and light.

The music is swinging; people are up and singing praises, floating on the energy between altar and drums. Candles glimmer on silver cloth. I smell them, brightness and heat. And it comes on me: the gut-falling, tunnel-vision so-relaxed exhilaration that presages these times of God coming forth through folks. Elegba, firmly in his "horse"—a possessed devotee—parades and pirouettes before the drums: rum and tobacco, and wet new leaves.

Now Red is up and leading the chorus, standing before the drummers and gesturing to heaven and earth, imploring in Spanish and Lukumi. Here comes a rush: I keep my feet— the tingle is small, in my lower back and lower belly—and all around, sweat is rolling, muscles coiling, voices calling, someone's, someone's . . . someone's gonna . . . Yes! I can feel it! My ears ! Sound's silver now, now gold, now shimmering brass, now clanging steel . . . That's *my* bell, keep it strong . . .

Drums boom—I feel them hit the floor. The pace is getting wild and tight, the energy pierces, compresses the air like an atom bomb, and here comes the voice of the one the energy takes this time. It's a woman, a high burst, then a cooling, cooling moan: the sound of giving it up to God . . . Here she comes . . . There! Hands are up, they're spinning, they're spinning; her eyes are closed, her feet twirl to the altar, she bends and snuffs no candle. She backs up and prostrates herself before it. Ritually assisted to her feet, she steps back, then twirls again to a half-step in front of the drums and Stop! And go again, and Martin's right with her, poppin' and slappin' and bassin' that drum to curl and fuse the sound into a tunnel that leads all life force to that one dancer, the one that's open to the wavelengths of God, and who's willing to be the mouthpiece, to take the weight, and stand for people's need.

And then there's another! A different devotee in white:

this one comes at us with shaking shoulders and clenched-tight eyes. Priest steps forward with a mouth full of empowered liquor and sprays it across the initiate's face and upper body. Devotee shoots up, standing straight, silent, and is taken by the hand to be dressed in the God's accoutrements and walk among the devoted, spreading the Power and the word of God today.

And I'm here, head back, eyes open, knees flexed, breathing deep, watching, watching, watching it all, still playing: discerning who is blessed, who is cleared of the Spirit. What colors, what drink, what tools the deities carry. How the songs affect them. How the drums empower them, how it is they dance. Who it is they see the need to counsel. How do they see? The ritual rolls on and on. I feel it, I feel it. I feel it.

I'm off the bell—Phil plays—and now I'm free to move. The ringing in my ears changes from a roar to a rush as I move from behind the drums. I follow in the dance, taking steps from those most fluid. Throughout, the Orisha drape arms across people's shoulders, and give advice to folks about their lives, their knowns and unknowns; some nod, some shake, some freeze. The chorus continues, empowering, enabling, reminding.

And, in its midst, I step back. Now, in this place, where am I? Unknown to these folks, untied to this culture; yeah, true: but I'm in it, it's in me. What do I do with this God energy? Where do I put this light? Who *should* I give this to, share this feeling with? Even: Should I feel this? Where am I allowed?

I look up. Ten feet away, the woman Obatalá has taken; chestnut tan, mid-thirties, brusque and solid, in an olive-green dress with the God's white cloth thrown over her shoulders. She is looking at me. Leaning way back, arms crossed . . . she looks at me. And sees me, knows my . . . takes my thought, my questions. And slowly, slowly, smiles.

I can't take this; I'm *seen*. Like laser through a balloon, like a yearling trapped in headlights, I'm made! Spotted, cold! Stripped naked! And still she softly smiles. And steps, and steps, steps closer. Leans in and puts her anointed head to mine, up close to smell the person and the cloth and the Power and the drum and the smoke and the oil and the world . . . Her arms go 'round me, pull me in.

My arms are up and around, now, too, sharing the embrace. The calmness of the God entombs me, and I submit. I go with it, absorb the embrace to its fullest: in my head, my face, my chest, my arms; it rolls down my body and weighs me, lifts me from my body as it sinks. Obatalá is with me, right here, right now, correct.

I'm on the floor. *On the floor*. It's peace to me, around me, in me, this place of beginnings. That's where babies start. The truth is like that: humble, and quiet, and low. Seen by those with eyes to see.

The God steps back, now done. I get up. And, swear to God, I do not remember right after then. I looked for the Deity, saw lights and flowers and cloth of the altar. I saw the smile. I saw me quiet, inside. Quiet.

Later on, after much hard playing, Otello danced and gave up his body to the deity that ruled his head. Strange, I thought, that it took the priest so long a time to possess. Anointed and dressed in his vestments, he counseled—I remember how he said what he did: with an elder's quiet vehemence and concern for the children, gesturing with one arm while with the other holding close the counselee. He counseled Red, I remember. I watched that, too. But I was done. I'd asked of God that day, God had come. God allowed me to feel the place to be, for me. I thank you, Those From Before, and the Great Mystery. I share my energy, today, that the Great Work be done.

PICASSO'S WORLD
AND THE
AFRICAN
CONNECTION

WARREN M. ROBBINS

W arren M. Robbins was born in Worcester, Massachusetts. He received an MA in history from the University of Michigan. Dr. Robbins served in the United States Information Agency (USIA) in Germany and Austria from 1950 to 1960. While there, he became interested in African art. He resigned from USIA in 1962, and in 1964, he established the first museum in the United States devoted to the heritage, culture, and art of Africa. In 1978, Congress passed legislation merging the museum with the Smithsonian Institution and establishing the National Museum of African Art in Washington, DC.

Dr. Robbins is the author of the two-volume *African Art in American Collections*, as well as many articles on art, science, and culture. He is the recipient of the Smithsonian Institution's Joseph Henry Medal, the Aggrey Medal of the Phelps Stokes Fund, Houston's Rothko Chapel Medal for Dedication to Truth and Freedom, and a Distinguished Service Award from the Hubert H. Humphrey Institute of Public Affairs. He was awarded an Honorary Doctorate from the University of New Hampshire.

Dr. Robbins lives in Washington, DC, where he serves as Director Emeritus and Senior Scholar of the National Museum of African Art.

Since the first decade of this century, the art of pre-industrial, non-Western cultures, primarily African, has had an undeniable and increasingly apparent impact on the Western aesthetic. One can find evidence of African influence in the principal art movements of twentieth-century Europe and America—German Expressionism, Fauvism, Cubism, Surrealism, Futurism—as well as reverberations in contemporary developments.

This influence was transmitted subtly via the Moorish culture of North Africa and Spain. Pablo Picasso's mother was Arabic; Picasso once declared to André Malraux: "I am a brother of the Black Fetishists." It was also conveyed with the "souvenirs" that sailors, explorers, colonizers, missionaries, or ethnologists brought back from Africa, many of which eventually found their way into the ethnological museums and curio shops of Europe. The influence of traditional African sculpture upon Western art has been pervasive both in form and design and at deeper levels of the aesthetic concepts behind the art.

Scholars steeped in the restricted traditions of European art have finally begun to take note of aesthetic relationships between Western and non-Western art, if not yet to acknowledge the full extent to which Western art has drawn literally and liberally from other cultures. Others have recognized this influence with greater conviction. *Time* magazine art critic Robert Hughes, for example, went so far as to state in *The Shock of the New* that Picasso plundered African art. Hughes likened Cubism to a "dainty parody of the imperial model. The African carvings," he wrote, "were an exploitable resource, like copper or palm-oil, and Picasso's use of them was a kind of cultural plunder."

Some today in the field of art history pass the subject off as old hat. Others seek to uphold modern artists' reputation for originality by denying the significance of what I would term the "cultural imperialism" of Africa on the waning creativity of end-of-the-century Europe. But for many more people—the vast numbers of bewildered and curious patrons of the museums of twentieth-century art—the discovery of the catalytic role of so-called primitive art has been a revelation.

The first scholarly investigation of the relationship of the two art forms was a book published in 1938, *Primitivism in Modern Painting* by Professor Robert Goldwater of New York University, who served subsequently as director of Nelson Rockefeller's Museum of Primitive Art before it became part of the Metropolitan Museum of Art. But the relationship between non-Western art and Western art did not begin to attract much public attention until 1948 when the Institute of Contemporary Arts in London mounted the exhibition "40,000 Years of Modern Art." Subsequently, a number of smaller shows were exhibited in Germany and elsewhere.

Then in 1972, the exhibition "World Cultures and Modern Art" was mounted in Munich in conjunction with the Olympic Games. The exhibition addressed the assimilation of Asian influences into the Western visual and performing arts. One section of this exhibition, organized by Manfred Schneckenberger, focused on the arts of Africa, Oceania, and what Schneckenberger called "Indo-America."

Another significant step toward greater public understanding was a highly instructive 1981 exhibition, "Gauguin to Moore: Primitivism in Modern Sculpture," organized by Alan Wilkinson at the Art Gallery of Toronto. A modest display on the same theme, juxtaposing original graphics and lithographic reproductions of Western works with traditional African carvings, was maintained from 1967 to 1982 at the Museum of African Art in Washington, DC.

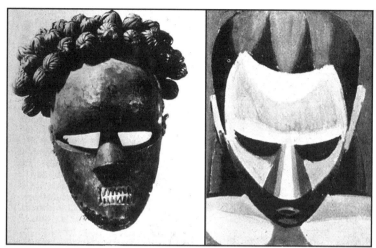

Salampasu people. Mask.

Pablo Picasso. Head of Man. Oil, 1908.

However, it was the 1984-85 exhibition "Primitivism in Twentieth Century Art—Affinity of the Tribal and the Modern" that caused public awareness of this issue to gain momentum. Shown at the Museum of Modern Art (MOMA) in New York and the Detroit and Dallas museums, this highly publicized exhibition was as controversial as it was dramatic; as much criticized—frequently for the wrong reasons—as it was praised. It featured a discriminating selection of the very finest examples of non-Western, particularly African, art to be found. As an unintended by-product, it brought home to the uninitiated viewer how far superior many of the African objects were to the Western works with which they were juxtaposed. It was perhaps the most important exhibition of African art *per se* that had ever been assembled.

The exhibition dealt primarily with the remarkable *affinities* between revolutionary works by Western artists, conceived and viewed in a strictly aesthetic context, and the highly disciplined traditional works of tribal carvers, made and utilized in a spiritual, intellectual, and aesthetic realm far from that of the Western world. What the exhibition did not succeed in doing, however, was to reflect adequately the extent of *direct derivation* from African art in so many of the Western works represented in the show. This shortcoming was perhaps a result of a scholarly distrust of the "merely visible" and too great a readiness to dismiss what were regarded as "banal resemblances" as being of little or no significance. A number of the works that were included in the MOMA exhibition to suggest direct influence were justifiably criticized as being too much a matter of conjecture to be convincing—this despite the fact that there was and is an abundance of irrefutable examples of forms and ideas directly derived from African art that can be drawn upon for purposes of illustration.

The significance of direct derivation from African forms has been played down not so much because of the real danger of

Tabwa people, Zaire. Female figure.   *Max Pechstein, German*
Expressionist. Woodcut, 1919.

*Top left: Senufo people, Cote
d'Ivoire. Detail, head of figure. Top
right: Max Pechstein, German
Expressionist. Woodcut, 1920.
Bottom: Roy Lichtenstein.
Woodcut, 1980.*

attributing to African art borrowings that actually derive from other facets of the Western cultural tradition. Nor has it been so much because of the likelihood that the resemblances between African art and modern art are a result of historical coincidence—with key developments or discoveries occurring simultaneously in different parts of the world independently of one another.* Nor has direct derivation been ignored in favor of another explanation, psychologist Carl Jung's concept of the "collective unconscious," which holds that certain archetypal forms are universal, appearing in all cultures. In my opinion, direct derivation has been neglected because Western scholars and critics have been disinclined to investigate visual clues that would lead to documentation of a startling hypothesis: that the true source of so many aesthetic devices and ideas passed off as original in the Western frame of reference is African art.

The situation is complicated by the interdisciplinary nature of this field. Africanists, though intimately acquainted with the highly disciplined elemental nuances of African styles, are more concerned with their responsibility to record and evaluate African art and artifacts as physical manifestations of the customs and values of fast-disappearing cultures.

Western art historians, on the other hand, having only a superficial acquaintance with the stylistic elements and devices of African art, do not find what they do not know. Furthermore, they do not apply the same exacting standards to their investigations of non-Western art that they expect of themselves within the Western aesthetic tradition. They pass over and pass on, unwittingly, the historical inexactitudes that have been put forth at various times, for various reasons,

---

*Pierre Daix, a leading historian of Cubism and personal friend of Picasso, attributed certain similarities between Cubist art and African art to "chance resemblances" and wrote an essay entitled "There Is No Negro Art in 'Les Demoiselles d'Avignon,'" referring to Picasso's controversial painting. He later recanted the opinion expressed in that article.

Mossi people, Burkina Faso. Detail, antelope mask.

Henry Moore. Sculpture, Large Totem Head, 1968.

by historians, critics, or artists themselves. Thus they give compounded credence to them through repetition. Meanwhile they often ignore statements such as that of Picasso's roommate and intimate friend the poet Max Jacob, who said "Cubism was born of Negro art." Maurice de Vlaminck, reputedly the first "discoverer" of African art among the European artists, wrote: "The so-called renaissance of modern art is nothing more than a bastard arrangement of Negro art. In order to recover their youth, the elect of our civilization who no longer have anything to say, have grasped greedily at the art of these alleged savages . . ." André Derain, co-founder along with Vlaminck and Henri Matisse of the art movement called Les Fauves (The Wild Beasts), bought the now famous *Fang* mask from Vlaminck for fifty francs. Regarding this mask, Derain said: "Picasso has seen my Negro mask. As soon as he returned home, he copied it. He is aware of everything; he copied everything. The greatest creator of forms of this century is an imitator."

There is, of course, far more to be said about the complicated relationship of the two art forms and, more importantly, about what was done with ideas and devices appropriated from African art. Therein lies one aspect of the significance of the modern art movements: Each of them taught us to perceive our inherited environment in new and nonhabitual ways and to understand better the intellectual evolution of the human being.

Traditionally and invariably, the principal criterion for establishing the fact of direct derivation in the field of art has been historical documentation—the artist owned a particular object or saw it in a museum or even in a book. *Might have seen* is not enough. But in the absence of documentation, when a substantial number of specific stylistic elements or devices are present in a single Western work, or a characteristic African style exists in a series of works by a particular Western artist—that, I maintain, constitutes what in a court of law would be termed "demonstrable evidence." If the visual clues are unique or numerous enough, they should hold up in the court of art history and the conclusions to be drawn from them should be deemed valid. Valid, that is, until such time as it can be demonstrated conclusively that a certain object could not have been a source of derivation because it—or even a picture of it—*could not have been present* in Europe at the time a Western art work was created. The evidence of directly derived forms constitutes what Juan Gris, co-inventor along with Picasso and Georges Braque of Cubism, called "signposts along the way," pointing directly to African sculpture on the road traveled toward modern art.

To acknowledge that so many early modern artists drew heavily and literally from African art does not necessarily denigrate their contributions to modern art and to modern understanding. For in so drawing, they translated it into their own work, interpreting it aesthetically with their own visual statements. Thus, such artists have served in effect as visual ethnohistorians.

Nor does heavy borrowing necessarily detract from the genius of modern artists. Who is to deny the genius of Picasso—who probably drew upon everything that he ever saw to feather his own aesthetic nest. (His very name "Picazo," as it was spelled in Arabic, means "magpie.") Perhaps Picasso's uncanny ability to take in and reconstruct for his own purposes forms drawn from all cultures is the true manifestation of his very genius. He was a synthesizer of untold sensitivity and vision.

All art is, of course, derivative—either from nature, or from prior art. Direct derivation is not only unavoidable but perfectly legitimate. In fact, there is today a school of art known as "appropriation art." What is done with what is derived determines whether an artist's work is significant, and that is up to the aestheticians to debate—if not to decide.

Lega people, Zaire. Mask.

Paul Klee. Maid of Saxony. Oil, 1922.

In not recognizing or acknowledging directly derived forms, art historians and critics fall short in their responsibility to help keep each age informed and conversant with the past. But even more important today—when crosscultural awareness and understanding become vital for survival— they fail to keep us apprised of the universal creativity of humankind in whatever culture and form it finds expression.

IEMANJÁ,
THE SEA QUEEN
MOTHER

ZECA LIGIERO
AND
PHYLLIS GALEMBO

P hyllis Galembo was born in New York City. She is an associate professor in the Department of Art at The State University of New York, Albany.

Ms. Galembo's photography has been exhibited at the International Center for Photography in New York. Her photographs are also included in several collections, among them the Schomburg Center for Research in Black Culture, the National Museum of African Art and the Metropolitan Museum of Art. Ms. Galembo is the author of *Pale Pink* and *Divine Inspiration: From Benin to Bahia*. She has been awarded several grants.

Ms. Galembo lives in New York City.

Z eca Ligiero was born in Rio de Janeiro. He received a master's degree in performance studies from New York University, where he is currently a PhD candidate.

Mr. Ligiero is a director and a playwright. He received the Mambembinho director's award in Rio de Janeiro and was founder and director of the graduate department of drama at the Federal University of Rio de Janeiro. He is the author of several books published in Brazil and was a contributor to *Divine Inspiration: From Benin to Bahia*. His work has appeared in several journals.

Mr. Ligiero lives in New York with his wife, Ana Cristina Coelho, and their two children, Yan and Yara.

(. . .)
I am going to ask permission
I am going to the sea
The brightness of the day
will shine me, oooo

I will swim
I will dive in the waters
And purify myself
At the bottom of the ocean
on the caprice of Janaina
The purity of the sea
Oh Queen Mother Iemanjá.

"Oloan," a song by Afro-Brazilian composer Wilson Moreira, captures the importance of the Yoruba goddess Yemoja in Brazil. There she is known also as Iemanjá or Janaina. According to the mythology of the Yoruba people of West Africa, Yemoja transformed herself into a river, and so represents the principle of movement and of passivity, characteristic of both springwater and the ocean. In Brazil she is solely associated with the ocean, but she occupies a very important position in the Afro-Brazilian pantheon: She is the mother of all other deities, or *orixás*. As ocean, Iemanjá links old Africa, whence symbolically she sprang, with the newborn African Americans. In fact, the two major Brazilian celebrations for Iemanjá are held on the shores of Salvador (in the state of Bahia) and Rio de Janeiro, Brazil's two largest geographical centers of African heritage. The beauty and deep spiritual meaning of these festivals have made them the most popular and widely celebrated in the Americas. Iemanjá's public celebrations focus on self-purification and renewal.

Yoruba religion was one of the religions carried to Brazil by Africans. The first African slaves were brought to Brazil by the Portuguese in 1538 and over the next three hundred years, Brazil received slaves from various African regions that would later be known as Angola, Guinea, Senegal, Ivory Coast, Ghana, Togo, Congo, and Mali. But it was not until 1830 that very large numbers of Yoruba were imported to serve the Portuguese as slaves. Many members of the traditional Yoruba kingdom—high priests and priestesses, artisans, and blacksmiths—had the same captive destiny, and most were sent to the same region, the city of Salvador and the surrounding cocoa farms in the state of Bahia.

Until that time, slave owners had made a point of separating people who spoke the same language and in so doing weakened cultural ties. When the Yoruba arrived in Brazil, for the first time a large group of Africans who came from one place and shared a complex culture were allowed to stay together, sharing tents and slave quarters. There the resilience of their culture became evident. Only a few years after their arrival, because of their skills and knowledge, many Yoruba had earned enough by working on the side to buy their freedom and the freedom of their people.

The focus of Yoruba cultural resistance in Brazil was the Candomblé houses, sacred spaces set apart for a wide range of rituals and worship of the *orixás*. Within Candomblés the environment of an African village was recreated and ancient Yoruba performances were resurrected, including the traditional songs and dances of the *orixás*. In addition, according to Yoruba philosophy, the many manifestations of the forces of nature constitute aspects of the *orixás*. For the Yoruba in Brazil, forest, sea, wind, thunder, stones, river, and so forth were also seen as divine altars.

In Africa, Iemanjá is depicted as a voluptuous, buxom African woman with a shapely derriere; in the New World, she is represented by two Western images: the mermaid and the Virgin Mary. In the New World, black images could not be used in rituals because of the high risk of persecution practiced by the Brazilian authorities during the colonial period. Later, because Africans were forbidden to practice their religion openly, the original African statues were replaced with Catholic imagery. Africans cloaked their worship of the *orixás* by identifying them with Catholic saints. The main characteristics of Iemanjá were diffused on new white images—coolness and high spirituality as found in the Virgin Mary, and fertility and attractive power associated with the mermaid.

The Latin form of the mermaid in this case does not have the devilish characteristics attributed to it by Europeans and Native Americans. On the contrary, she is very positive and the guardian of fishermen. For instance, in one city in Bahia, a statue of Iemanjá protects a *colonia de pesca*, or fishermen's community house. She holds her traditional round mirror, an object she uses to admire her own beauty. Necklaces and bracelets are regularly replaced on her statue, the new ornaments being proof of believers' renewed faith and love for her. An added crown of flowers adorns her very spiritual head. Within a nearby Candomblé house, Iemanjá's image is painted on the wall. She is pictured resting on rocks, which, according to Yoruba religion, are symbols of immortality. The image juxtaposes the transitory and the eternal. At the gateway to Terreiro Ze Ogum, or shrine to Ogum, Iemanjá assumes human features in the statue, welcoming visitors. Dressed as a priestess, Iemanjá mirrors her devotees, who give her flowers and gifts. The star atop her head indicates her transcendent spirituality. And when Iemanjá comes to earth in human form in a trance, she wears a very elaborate costume: a silver crown with beaded fringes, silver bracelets, and a spangled skirt reminiscent of ocean waves. When she dances, her body recreates the constant undulating balance of the sea. She carries a silver sword in her left hand, assuring her power over the water kingdom.

Celebrations in honor of Iemanjá are always major events. In Salvador, there are two of them: Festa para Iemanjá (Feast for Iemanjá) and Presentes para Iemanjá (Gifts for Iemanjá). The Feast for Iemanjá occurs on the day the Roman Catholic calendar dedicates to the Virgin Mary of the Immaculate Conception. This celebration has become very syncretic, attracting both Catholic and Candomblé worshipers.

The church consecrated to the Virgin Mary of the Immaculate Conception is one of the best known in Salvador and a special place visited by fishermen. The procession is at the center of the festivities. The majority of participants of predominantly African descent wear white Candomblé liturgical garments. Afro-Brazilian drums are played. The grounds around the church are decorated with colorful lights and banners, and hundreds of wooden booths ornamented with images of the *orixás* and Catholic saints are built. Vendors sell food, seasonal fruits, soda, refreshments, and alcoholic beverages.

On February 2, Presentes para Iemanjá is organized by traditional Candomblé houses, each of which has a shrine. The day before the celebration, gifts are set before Iemanjá's shrine in order to receive her blessings. Early the next morning private rituals take place in numerous Candomblé houses. The devotees enter Iemanjá's room, sing, and ask her protection. Then they pick up their gifts and, balancing them carefully on their heads, walk in procession toward the nearest beach. Their steps trace an imaginary line between the shrine and the ocean. This follows the pattern of Iemanjá's original ritual in Yorubaland, where devotees bear offerings of Iemanjá's favorite food, boiled white corn mixed with sea-nut butter, and wooden sculptures of her human image. They carry these on their heads as they travel to the source of the Ogum River spills into the Atlantic Ocean, where Iemanjá is supposed to have changed herself into a river.

The next part of the ceremony is held on the shore, where on other days of the year fishermen weigh their daily catch. Sympathetic people of different classes and races join the Candomblé's procession on the shore. Awaiting Iemanjá's blessings, they too bring gifts: flowers in white or pastel colors, combs, mirrors, soaps packed in transparent wrappers, dolls, perfumes, dishes—everything that a beautiful and vain woman might enjoy. The people gather as many gifts as possible in *cestas*, huge wicker baskets, which will be placed on boats and carried to sea for Iemanjá; notes of thanks or requests for love and money accompany each gift. Some of the devotees prefer going directly into the water to offer their presents personally. Meanwhile, the crowds near the shore have fun, screaming with laughter, greeting Iemanjá. Many small ships and rafts form a convoy to the high sea, where the *cestas* are released into the depths of the ocean. According to tradition, if the gifts sink, Iemanjá has accepted them; if they return to the shore with the tide, it is because she has refused them. A very similar celebration occurs in Rio de Janeiro, where the celebration for Iemanjá is held on New Year's Eve.

In public celebrations to Iemanjá, believers find an open space for approaching their deity. While in everyday life Iemanjá is personified as a mermaid or even a Catholic saint, in her public ceremonies she returns to her original element: water. And, through the miracle of faith, Iemanjá purifies each believer for next year's journey. All the heavy suffering of each year is made tolerable through Iemanjá's belly—only she can transform sorrow into happiness and give birth to a better life in the coming year.

Devotees who travel out to the high sea in a boat evidence commitment to her wisdom. In worship it is possible to understand how Iemanjá encompasses the traits of a great lover as well as a great mother. She is seen as an open shell who shelters beauty and reveals compassion, and as a sacred pearl who brings fertility and love.

Iemanjá protects the fishermen's community house in Rio Vermelho beach, Salvador.

Iemanjá as mermaid in a Candomblé house.

Iemanjá appears to her followers through a priestess in a trance.

Iemanjá as priestess in Terreiro Ze Ogum.

Devotees in Iemanjá's room.

Devotees carry gifts to the shore.

Gifts for Iemanjá.

Transporting the gifts to the sea.

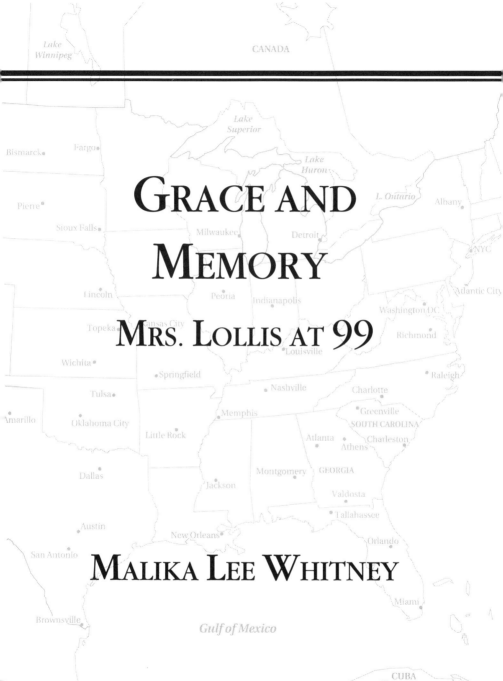

GRACE AND MEMORY

MRS. LOLLIS AT 99

MALIKA LEE WHITNEY

Malika Lee Whitney was born in Harlem of Jamaican parentage. The author of *Bob Marley: Reggae King of the World*, she is an educator and radio producer and host. In addition, Ms. Whitney is artistic director of Pickney Productions and the Pickney Players. As a performing artist and storyteller, she has been seen extensively on stage and television and in film. Ms. Whitney is affectionately known by thousands of children as Peenywally. She is an artist in residence with Community Works and City Lore, the Center for the Study of Urban Folklore.

Ms. Whitney divides her time between Jamaica and Harlem.

Mary Lou Lollis was born in Greenville, South Carolina. A traditional storyteller, Mrs. Lollis has been featured on many radio programs broadcast by Pacifica Radio, WLIB, WNYC, and National Public Radio. She has shared her stories with schoolchildren and with young and adult audiences at festivals, libraries, and cultural institutions throughout the northeastern United States.

Mrs. Lollis, who lives in New York City, turned 99 years old on January 1, 1994.

If no use were made of the labor of the ages, the world would remain in the infancy of knowledge. So said historian Carter G. Woodson. It is in the quest for knowledge, understanding, and perhaps the meaning of life that we turn to those most experienced in living, our esteemed elders.

The survival of our culture, heritage, and social history is largely dependent on how we care for and obtain information from these most cherished citizens.

I met Mary Lou Lollis at a bus stop where Central Park begins for Harlemites. I remember being intrigued by the life lines in her face. My next thought sprang to one of concern. I wondered what she was doing out on the street alone. I chanced an introduction, knowing the cautious nature of some of our elders toward strangers. Not surprisingly, her face lit up with a beautiful smile, and she replied politely and in a most refined way, "I'm Mary Lou Lollis." While we waited for the bus we made conversation, starting with the basic slowness of service of public transportation and the weather. We moved to other topics quickly, and with every response I could sense that this smartly dressed, diminutive woman was a repository of something very rich, very special—something she wanted to share. The ride was a short one for me, and after she had assured me that she was quite all right, we parted. I left her my card and promised that I would get in touch with her very soon. Thoughts of her stayed with me for many days. As one deeply involved in the study of oral traditions and folklore, I knew that Mrs. Lollis was like the woman Langston Hughes wrote about in his poem "Aunt Sue's Stories." History was in her head. Mrs. Lollis in fact made the first of several calls to me, waging a battle with technology and answering machines until we made that most important link. It is a link that remains, for since that time her stories have never ceased to flow.

*   *   *

Malika Lee Whitney: We begin, I guess, on the day of your arrival. Your life starts with a kind of special entrance into the world. Can you tell us about that day?

Mary Lou Lollis: Well, in view of the fact that I might have been looking everywhere but I couldn't say anything, I was told by my mother and father and my grandmother and my aunts who were all present, the doctor, it was January 1, 1895, at 1:00 am, New Year's morning.

MLW: Where in the United States was that?

MLL: Greenville, South Carolina. I was born of a mother

who had at one time been a slave. She was ten years old by the time Mr. Lincoln came along and gave them their supposed freedom. My grandmother had ten children, and the older ones were born in slavery.

MLW: What do you remember about your childhood growing up in South Carolina? What recollections come to mind?

MLL: Well, I know as children we didn't have any hard time, but there were other children who were suffering all around us. My mother became a missionary for Springfield Baptist Church, our church. My grandfather had helped to build that church. My mother and whole family were members there. My mother was elected to be missionary because there was so much suffering in the community, and she went everywhere. Wherever she didn't reach, children and grown-ups that were suffering knew if they could get to Mrs. Alice Hall's house, they could get some kind of assistance. My mother went to the wealthy people of the city. People whose homes my father had helped to build, because he was a carpenter. Some of them were very rich people and some of them were just—I guess you would call them—there's another word for it but this is the one that comes to my mind—medium livers—(laughter), and they would always give her food and clothing and sometimes money. And she did that just as long as she lived, even after she came to New York after the death of my father.

We grew up in the public schools up to the fifth grade. My little cousin—the principal of that school hit him with a baseball bat. Even though my mother's and my grandmother's children, some of them were slaves, they had temper and they took him out of that public school, and my aunt sent her son to North Carolina and we were sent to Sterling College from the fifth grade up and I finished the ninth grade at Sterling College.

MLW: What was the cause of the principal striking your cousin with the bat?

MLL: Well, because one of the other students had done something very wrong to a student who was very much smaller and younger than he was, and he laid the guilt on my cousin. And even though my cousin strongly denied it and told them he was not guilty, the principal just sent a bunch of them into the closet where he administered his punishment. He hit my cousin because they all pointed at him. My mother had three children and I was the only one of my mother's children that would fight, and my aunt had three and she had one that was too young to fight back and the other one wasn't big enough, he was younger than any of us. So I had to fight back, and I told it like it was because I didn't see the boy hit him but some of the other children that were standing there watching it said it was not my cousin that put the licking on the other little boy, it was another boy. The kids for some reason were envious of us 'cause we—if I have to say so, it's the truth, so help me God—we went to school looking different to what they did because their parents didn't have jobs and they didn't have any income and the children were not properly clad—only some of those who other people (like my mother) had helped to get decent clothes to wear to school.

MLW: Since the telling of stories of people of African descent or people born in the South tends to be a tradition, are there any stories that you remember being told by your mother or your grandmother that maybe connected you with our African past or something that helped to give your family a sense of self, a sense of pride and dignity?

MLL: My grandmother took great pride in telling us of all the tribulations that she went through when she as a mother gave birth to so many children during slavery. My grandmother's father was Irish and my grandmother's mother was a full-blooded African woman. My grandmother was chosen to work in the house of this slave owner of whom she was a daughter. But she got a lot of cruel treatment although she was a member of that family. Her father and her slave owner didn't want his wife to know that she was his child, but she knew she belonged to some white man because my grandmother's mother was a black woman, a real full-blooded African woman. She had to do what that Irishman told her to do, and he had many on his plantation in the same situation and he tried to keep those women by whom he had gotten babies living somewhere on the plantation *not too far from him*. And if he saw fit to go to any one of the log huts and make . . . If any of them had tried to get married or were living with any man . . . If they had jumped over the broomstick to get married . . .

But there was always someone in the crowd that had sneaked into the house to their parents who was working in the house. And they would stay close enough to the white children, the slave owner's children. And those children didn't know anything about racism, only as it was taught to them by their parents, and before they became filled with it themselves they would teach some of those slave children how to read and write and how to count. And some of those slave children learned to read the Bible. And even though some of the adults had to jump over the broomstick, because slave masters told them that was sufficient marriage, some of those slave children that knew better would take them into the woods after midnight and take a candle and read that Bible and give them a Christian ceremony for marriage. That's one part of the cruelty.

And there were times when if that white man wanted to go into any one of them log huts and get in the bed with one of them women that he had called his own, that black man had to get out, whatever color he was. And Abraham Lincoln said he was tired of that kind of ill treatment and that's when he tried to free the people and possibly would have done more in that direction if they had let him live long enough. So I shall always respect him for what he did and honor his name and his birthday to the best of my ability. Our people in the South did that for the longest time, and they still do.

But when I came to New York I found out that the Republican Party [Lincoln's party] didn't mean anything anymore. Most of the people here, because of the Republicans, were so sour on the black people and they were working them, after they had brought them, like slaves, without any pay. Our people didn't know what pay was. All they had was cornbread and black molasses, black-eyed peas to eat Sunday and Monday and every other day in the week and no kind of pay to buy shoes or clothes or anything else. They gave them whatever kind of mess they wanted them to wear and that was that. And if they got food they had to go to the sharecropper's store and get it on credit. When harvest time came, they would say, "You owe it all for such and such a thing." And that was after Lincoln supposedly freed them. They still had to live on the white man's land and they had to (supposedly) pay rent. And they would take one part for rent, and the sharecropper's store would take the other part for the food. Now where did the clothes and shoes come from? They would throw them some old shoes, old brogans as they used to call them, and jeans. In those days, like when my father was a young man working every day, I never saw no jeans like they have now—red and blue and all other colors—they were black. My father used to work in black jeans. So it was suffering all those years for those people who were working to keep the house clean. They still got cruelty.

That old woman where my mother was kept a cat o' nine tails, and I guess the rest of them did. And if you did anything wrong, if they caught you eating food that you were not supposed to have, you got beat with the cat o' nine tails. One morning after my grandfather had taken his two sons—the oldest boys, and they were older than my mother—to the field with him, my mother was hungry and crying for bread. My grandmother said she was fixing to cook that cornbread but she had to be sure that she got some food fixed for the white folks first.

So she found one biscuit and she gave that to my mother and in the meantime this old white woman came out and saw my mother with a biscuit. My grandmother said my mother was between three and five years old, couldn't no longer remember the exact date of her birth but in later years it did come to her. And she said [mimicking tone of white woman] "Mary, I'm sorry but you gave that child a biscuit to eat and you know she not supposed to eat biscuits, she supposed to eat cornbread like the rest of you. I'll have to whip you, Mary." My grandmother cut all the meat and she cooked it and my grandmother knew as much about separating a animal—a calf and the cow and a hog or whatever they brought in there for her to cook. So she had a chopping block just like they have in the meat market, and around that chopping block was knives and she better have those knives sharp so she could cut anything they brought in there for her to cook. So while this woman went to get the cat o' nine tails, Grandma took two of those knives and began sharpening them. When she got back she was still sharpening them. [Imitating the white woman again] "Mary, what in the world you gonna do with them knives? I didn't come out here to tell you nothing to cook. I'm gonna whip you with the cat o' nine tails because if my husband finds out that that child was eating a biscuit he'll want to do something to you hisself and he hit you harder than I will." My grandmother said, If you come over here and hit me with that cat o' nine tails, I'll chop you head off—Grandma said the window had been open a little bit and she opened it wide—and let your head fly out the window. She said, "Mary, are you out of your mind?" She said, no, I'm not. Then she said, "Well, I'll whip the child." Then she said, If you touch my baby I'll kill you. I'll come over there and chop your head off and pick it up and throw it out the window. She said, "Well, you need to be bled." In those days, they would stick a needle, a nail, a sharp knife or anything, right in that big vein and let you bleed till they got tired of seeing the blood or until they saw you gonna faint or something, my grandma said. Then they'd put some kind of plaster on, something that would stick, and that was your punishment. Sometimes the slaves would get so sick they would have to take them to the doctor. So [continuing to mock white woman] she said, "Well, I'll have to go and get your boss and get him to bleed you." So the husband came out to get a look at her and he had the cat o' nine tails in his hand and he said, "Mary, you been very sassy to your mistress and why don't I just give you a few licks with this cat o' nine tails and not bleed you?" Grandma said, If you hit my child, or come over here and hit me, I'll cut your head off and let *it* fly out the window and if it hits the floor, I'll pick it up and throw it out the window and I'll come over there and get your wife's head too. Don't touch my child and don't touch me either. Enough is enough and I've had enough and I don't intend to take any more. So that was the end of the cat o' nine tails with my grandmother, and they never came after her with the cat o'nine tails anymore.

MLW: There is a real gleam in your eye when you talk about your grandparents and the love and care that they showed. Maybe you can share another one of those wonderful stories that made you have such a deep and lasting love for them.

MLL: My grandmother and my mother were very much alike in their dispositions. Both were very kind-hearted people, and I was told that my grandfather was likewise.

Six children had been left standing on the road while their mother and father were sold to some slave owners who came all the way from Texas and didn't want the children, only the mother and the father. Those children, six boys, were left standing in the road crying. My grandfather told them to go up to the house. They were right in sight of my grandmother's and grandfather's little cottage where they stayed. He told my grandmother to make pallets and take them in, let them sleep, and the next morning after he got up and started out for the field or wherever he was going for his day of work, he said, "Mary, don't let them go, keep them. They haven't got anywhere to go and if they have to sleep on a pallet on the floor every night in the week, that's better than being out in the street with no food to eat and nowhere to sleep and nobody to love them." So my grandmother kept them. And they worked in the field with my grandfather and his children, and when my grandfather's four sons and that six that he had adopted unto himself (and my grandmother), when they all got to be teenagers and tired of going with the soles of their shoes hanging off and never any new clothes to wear and always there was a harvest and they saw him get money but they knew he had to give up the money, so the six boys—some of them were older than my grandfather's sons—so they all got together and decided to run away and they ran away and some of them never returned home. The oldest son of my grandmother returned once to see his mother, and I was a little girl then, just a child I would say, and my sister and brother likewise. And my mother's youngest brother didn't go far away, he only went to Asheville, North Carolina, and the other brothers went to Kansas and worked in the coal mines at night and went to school in the day. One became a minister of the gospel because he could study in the day when he finished high school and started studying for the ministry and became a Baptist minister but he never came back home but once. The younger one who lived in Asheville, after he finished growing up, he came often to visit my grandmother because he had a job as a janitor at the Vanderbilt Hotel in Asheville. My mother had taught him while she was growing up in the public schools.

The slaves had pooled their money to build a log cabin school, that's the only kind of houses they they had to live in—log cabins. They built this school and they pooled their money together and sent to new Hampshire and got a teacher. She taught them a little bit of French, she gave them music lessons, taught them how to sing, and she taught them up to the time that they dismissed her. But when the white people saw fit to build schools, after Lincoln supposedly freed them, they had up to the eighth grade. If you finished the eighth grade, you could go to college. My mother finished the eighth grade and she only went to college one year. That was Benedict College, which had only one room at that time.

MLW: In the lives of young people, there's usually some unpleasant things that they experience; in fact, many unpleasant things. What was it for you as a child that made you know or have some understanding of what racism in the South was all about?

MLL: Because they hated black people . . .

MLW: When you say they, "they" who?

MLL: The white people who were in the South. They were not born and reared there, they all had migrated there so they could have slaves and get rich, which they did. And they hated black people and I *hated* them. But my mother was a devout Christian and so was my grandmother, but my grandmother had hatred in her heart for them for all the cruelty they had given out to her and her children . . . to her older children.

After my mother became an attractive young woman and got married to my father, by that time my grandfather had given up the farm because all the boys ran away, his four and the other six. He gave up the farm and with the little money he had managed to keep he moved in to what was considered suburbs. There they lived until they tried to buy a piece of property. Each time they tried to buy a farm, whatever money they paid down on it, it was accepted as the payment. They went back thinking that they could pay a little more and eventually they could move in there, but only to be reminded that that wasn't enough [money]. When my grandmother told us about that, I was so angry with everybody that I saw was white, but all the people that I saw were not responsible for that particular family, some of them were, but not at all. I hated the white ones just like they hated us.

MLW: Tell us what experiences you had *directly* that made you feel this way?

MLL: My grandfather started buying this place. My mother and her youngest sister helped and my mother did the most of it and he in his will, he fixed it so that she would get the largest lot, and my father built a little log hut on it for my mother and the first part of their family, and as they had more children every time my father would add another room. We ended up with a six-room cottage.

My father built toys for us. All of our toys were home-made, and white and black children came into our yard to play because we had a billy goat, my brother had a goat and pigeons and a puppy, and we had chickens, turkeys, guineas, ducks, and swings, push swings, and a two-seated wood swing under a shade tree, and the children were welcome from all over the community. White and black. And when this one particular little white boy would get angry if he couldn't have his way, he would call anybody that was close by him a *nigger* and then he belonged to me. Because I had heard that word and I looked it up in the dictionary and I found out that it didn't mean what the white man thought it meant. It meant a low-down dirty person and anybody can be that. And I knew there was plenty of them that should be called that and not our people, because our people were humble and worked hard and didn't bother nobody but they tried to defend themselves and didn't have enough things to properly defend themselves and so they were in lots of trouble. But I had no fear. I'd stand up there, rap on that little boy, I didn't care if . . . who came after me after that. And I felt I had vengeance on him 'cause I knew my grandmother had been beaten by some of his foreparents and if he could call me something that I knew I wasn't or any of the rest of the black children that played in our yard, I thought he ought to be beat and I beat him.

MLW: I know that you have been living in New York for more than six decades; what prompted your move up South?

MLL: I got married at the age of eighteen. My husband was a finished bricklayer. It was hard for black men with trades to get jobs in the town where we lived. And he had to so many times go out of town to work and he didn't like that. Didn't like leaving me. And then when we started a family, he liked it even less. Our children were all born there in Greenville, South Carolina. But when I lost the first ones—the first child didn't live, it was too large and had to be so badly bruised, the second one likewise—then I had to go on a special diet. My husband had a sunstroke the next year and I didn't have a baby that year. But then I had a miscarriage and then the next baby that I had, I had been on a diet and she was smaller and she came out without being bruised and lived. And then I had another child and she lived, and then a miscarriage and one miscarriage after I came to New York. Had all my children lived, I would have seven. As of now I have two girls, Ruby and Alice. I wanted my children to have the best of everything like we had as far as my mother and father could go. I liked New York very much because he got regular work and before he came he joined the international union so he could go anywhere to work. And he worked right here in New York City on the first job he had for eight years for the first contractor that hired him and would have worked continuously but he [the contractor] went out of business. He [the contractor] sold all of his machinery because he was getting old and he had been in business long before we came to New York. My husband earned more money and could take care of his family in a much better way. We had a better place in which to live and I liked New York very much for a lot of reasons. Whenever we went to a store, you could get waited on, we could pick the kind of places we wanted to live in and be accepted if we could pay for it, most of the time. But even here in New York City, there were places that had signs out, *no children and no Negroes allowed.* Just like in Greenville, South Carolina. Well, we learned to avoid those places and we found nice places that didn't operate in that way. And so I decided that all people were not alike, not in any nationality, and I learned to get along with people of all nationalities because I didn't know then that in later years I would be working with people who were from all nationalities.

MLW: You were here in New York at a time when it was very difficult to earn a livelihood. Were you able to assist your husband? Was his work so steady that you were able to be just a homemaker?

MLL: For a time it was. But then it looked to me like it was not gonna last so long, I was afraid . . . I didn't want to spend all of the little nest egg we had and a voice said to me, so plain I looked around, I thought somebody had entered my room, but no one was there. And the only thing I could think of was, that's God's spirit talking to me. "Create a job of your own." And I said, well, how can I do that? Then I said, oh I know what I'll do. I know how to cook and I'll make pies and cakes and sandwiches and sell to the school children. And I started and I had some money in the house, about $50, I guess. And I went out while my husband was in Long Island seeing about a job. I left my children with my best friend and I went out to Wisenbecker's and shopped for—with the little money I had—for some of the things that I needed to start with. And that afternoon, I put a card table down on the sidewalk and I had bought a brand-new mosquito net, I put a tablecloth on that table and I put a mosquito net to keep any flies or dust off to the best of my ability, and I had sandwiches and small pies and frankfurters and things that I knew schoolchildren would like downstairs. When my husband came he was shocked, and the school children crossed over the street when they saw it, and I told them that the next day I'd be selling lunches one flight up to the school children. And the children came and they were so tickled and some of then didn't even have money and they sat down at the table and said, "Mrs. Lollis, if you let me have something, my mother and father will send you the money tomorrow and if they don't have it tomorrow, when they get paid, Saturday they'll send it." I said, You sit right down with all those that have got money and I'll serve you just like I serve the rest. And I did. And I kept it up as long as I served food.

And then people, collectors, they were out collecting insurance, and people out there selling things; they couldn't understand why all those children were crowding up here, and the police couldn't understand it. And they came up, and when they saw the food, they bought lunches and some of them would buy a pie, and buy the pan too so they could take it home, and go down to the next police headquarters and send their friends from down there up to my house, and then, when children were not coming around as much—

MLW: You mean when school closed?

MLL: When school closed, the children were out in the street and some of them went to camp, and some of them were off on vacation with their parents. I took the basket and started going to garages and pool rooms and anywhere people were working, and I had gone occasionally before, but I went more after that, and on Election Day, I would always go to the school where they had polls. The caretaker would put a big canvas that he had over the piano there in the chapel, and I'd put my tablecloth over that and set the food on top of that, and I served people from that—the top of that piano, till finally they put a table in there for me. And then I started going to the beauty parlors, and one nice lady, Ms. Gibbs, a beautician, introduced me to one of her customers and that customer was none other than the first black woman that Cecil B. DeMille had on his movie screen, Eunice Brooks. She was really a real black star, and by going there and carrying my food, she—Ms. Gibbs—told me that she and her workers there in the beauty parlor would buy from me if I could come every day and so I did, and then one day a very great star came in and he was Cab Calloway. He said, "Say, what's all this you got around here?" and the beautician said, "You haven't seen anything." He saw the

117

people eating, but they had a table in the back, and they had curtains across, and she pulled the curtains back and she said, "You see that?" And I had all these pies, and ham, and rolls, and all the good things out. He said, "Lord have mercy," and Cab Calloway told others about it. The next time I came back I met Duke Ellington, I met Fats Waller. Fats Waller sang and he was an actor and a comedian, and there was another black man with a band, and I can't think of his name. Oh yes, Don Redman. Anyway, the crowd grew, and they started calling me "Pie Lady" in the pool room, and it got up to that beauty parlor. And they'd come and if the door was locked they'd say, "Is the Pie Lady there?" or "I hope she didn't leave yet," and they would buy food to take home, and the policemen would buy pies to take home. And when I started carrying apple pies—when I started carrying sweet potato pies, that did it. And so, black women that were in show business and black men that were in any type of show business, and the policemen and the school children helped me to make good money.

My husband, he couldn't stand to see me walk out the door with that basket; and my youngest daughter, Ruby, if she wasn't in school, she would go with me. The older one, Alice, and her father would stand at the window and cry; I could see the tears coming off of his eyes and in my older daughter's likewise, and the little one was there with me. And Cab Calloway used to put my little girl's money in one pocket, and my money in the other. She'd have a pocket full of money when we left and I'd have a pocket full of money, and Cab Calloway I don't think ever gave her less than fifty cents, and sometime he'd give her a dollar, sometime it wouldn't be but a quarter, and the others did likewise. When she'd get back home, Alice would say, "Ruby, let me help you take the money out of your pocket." She'd say, "Never mind, you won't go and help me and mother, so you just stand still, I'll get it out and don't touch this pocket over here; that's my money."

*   *   *

When I last visited Mrs. Lollis she was thinking about writing a letter to address the Clinton Administration. I already know how she'll punctuate it—the letter will be full of expressions of social reforms and her most important mandates—taking care of children and the elderly. Hopefully someone will listen; after all, she's been here, she ought to know.

PLAYING THE
DOZENS

JAMES PERCELAY,
MONTERIA IVEY, AND
STEPHAN DWECK

J ames Percelay is a writer and producer whose credits include production of parody commercials for "Saturday Night Live" and documentaries on subjects ranging from the Dance Theater of Harlem to the Rolling Stones. He was formerly head of development at Hearst Entertainment. Mr. Percelay is currently developing a television series for CBS.

Monteria Ivey is host and writer of the syndicated television series "Uptown Comedy Club" of Harlem and is host of that club's live shows. Mr. Ivey's recent performances include appearances on HBO's "Toyota Comedy Festival," "Comedy Central," and "Showtime at the Apollo."

Stephan Dweck is an attorney representing television and film actors and musical artists. He is general counsel for the National Black Theater and teaches entertainment law at Baruch College of CUNY.

Richard Majors is an assistant professor of psychology at the University of Wisconsin, Eau Claire.

The following selection, a portion of which was written by Richard Majors, is excerpted from *SNAPS!*, to be published in February by William Morrow.

The African-American game of "playing the dozens" is a comedic art form. Although it is older than jazz, this traditional game of insults is virtually unknown outside the African-American community. Born out of a shared experience of pain and prejudice, the repartee of the dozens remains almost a secret language. However, now that writers are starting to feature "mother jokes" in popular movies, commercials, and television shows, the game is headed for Main Street, USA.

Although the dozens is a comic art form, it is important to be aware of the pain from which this humor arises. The roughness of the verbal insults is an expression of those feelings. Ironically, the focus on "your mother" in so many snaps, or insults, points to a reverence most contestants have for their mother. In the dozens, this reverence is used as an emotional weapon.

The dozens is the blues of comedy. It is a ritual that crosses generational, regional, and class boundaries. The dozens illustrates the force of the spoken word and is the ultimate expression of fighting with your wits, not your fists.

African-American culture has often been called an oral culture, one rich in storytelling and verbal repartee. The dozens is one of the most interesting but least examined of these verbal traditions. It is a ritualized contest in which the object is to hurl insults at an opponent. The goal is to see which contestant can devise the most—and most effective—insults to humiliate the opposition. The loser is the one who backs down, runs out of snaps, or loses his cool, which occasionally results in a physical fight.

Some scholars trace the dozens to Africa. For example, author William Schechter reports that Ashanti natives often engage in verbal contests. And scholar Ram Desai writes that the worst offense a Gikuku tribesman could offer another is to "mention his mother's name in an indecent way."

However, author Middleton Harris in *The Black Book* ties the origin of the dozens to slavery. She suggests that auctioneers sold slaves individually, but those who were ill, old, or otherwise damaged goods were sold in lots of twelve. Hence the term "dozens."

Dan Burley, in Hubert Foster's *Ribbin', Jivin' & Playin' the Dozens*, also believed that the dozens originated during slavery, specifically with American field slaves who used the game in place of physical assault on higher-status house slaves. The field slaves knew they would be whipped or starved if they harmed the house slaves, so they vented their hostility by insulting the house slaves' parents and ancestors. The name "dozens," then, may have derived from the notion that the house slave's mother was "one of the dozens of women available to the sexual whims of her master."

Still other theories are proposed to explain the origin of the term "dozens." According to scholar Charles S. Johnson, the name may have originated from the unluckiness of throwing a twelve in craps. Scholar Roger Abrahams notes William Griffin's suggestion that it may derive from a definition of dozen: "to stun, stupefy, or daze." And jazz musician Johnny Otis recalls that "Dozens" was 1930s slang for a bawdy area of Kansas City known as Twelfth Street.

Young African-Americans play the dozens for entertainment and comedic value. However, research suggests that when slavery was legal in the United States the game helped one control anger and keep cool in white society. In *Ossie: The Autobiography of a Black Woman*, Ossie Guffy uses an anecdote to highlight the importance of the dozens as a strategy for self-control.

Ossie was born in 1931. She describes how she and four other children were playing on her grandfather's farm. One boy was hit and, instead of hitting back, started insulting the others with the dozens. Overhearing this, her grandfather lectured and paddled them:

"'When I was coming up,' Grandpa said, 'I heard about that game, only I heard about it the way it used to be, and I heard how it started and why it started. It was a game that slaves used to play, only they wasn't just playing for fun. They was playing to teach themselves and their sons how to stay alive. The whole idea was to learn to take whatever the master said to you without answering back or hitting him, 'cause that was the way a slave had to be, so he could go on living. It maybe was a bad game, but it was necessary. It ain't necessary now.'"

When Ossie's mother heard what had happened, she pointed out that although the boys should not have been using bad words, the game would teach them how to hold their tempers in check.

The emergence of the dozens in the popular media indicates its vitality. Played in movies like "White Men Can't Jump," "Bebe's Kids," and "Boomerang," the dozens has also been featured on "The Arsenio Hall Show," "Martin," "The Uptown Comedy Club," "Russell Simmons' Def Comedy Jam," "A Different World," and "In Living Color." Madison Avenue has been incorporating the dozens into commercials for Nike sneakers and Hallmark cards. It is unlikely that most viewers are aware that they demonstrate elements of a rich oral tradition.

This lack of awareness endangers that tradition's connection to the African-American culture. The dozens was conceived by a people who understood the need to create humor amidst adversity. Although the humor of the art form deserves to be shared, its cultural and linguistic value must be preserved. Maintaining the full spirit of the dozens demands keeping its clever prose attached to its bitter past.

*   *   *

You're so dumb, it takes you an hour-and-a-half to watch "60 Minutes."

You're so stupid, on the job application where it said "Sign here," you wrote "Aquarius."

You're so ugly, your family sent you to the store for bread, and then moved.

Your mother is so fat, she's on both sides of the family.
—from "Bebe's Kids"

Your brother is so stupid, he thought Boyz II Men was a daycare center.

You're so short, you have to cuff your underwear.
—Terry Hodges

Your mother is so old, she can read the Bible and reminisce.
—Hugh Moore

Your parents are so poor, they got married for the rice.

Your sister is so thin she sleeps in a pencil case.

You're so dumb, you think Beirut was a famous home-run hitter.

Your father is so fat, he got his baby pictures taken by satellite.

Your apartment is so small, when I put a key in the lock, I broke a window.

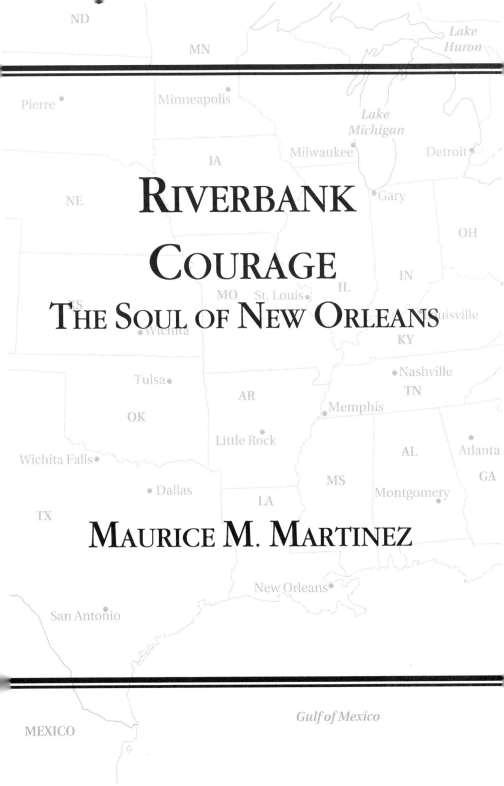

RIVERBANK

COURAGE

THE SOUL OF NEW ORLEANS

MAURICE M. MARTINEZ

Maurice M. Martinez was born in New Orleans. He holds a bachelor's degree from Xavier University and his master's degree and PhD from the University of Michigan. He received a Ford Foundation award to undertake two years of research in Brazil. Dr. Martinez is a professor in the Department of Educational Foundations at Hunter College, New York. He is the author of *School and Community: Issues and Alternatives* and *Education of Ethnic Minorities.*

Poet, photographer, musician, and filmmaker, Dr. Martinez produced the award-winning film documentary, "The Black Indians of New Orleans" in 1976. He directed and edited a series of videotapes entitled "Miserecords: Hidden Mirrors of Medieval Life" in 1992.

Dr. Martinez has written extensively on the Mardi Gras Indians. He is currently working on a history of the Black Indians of New Orleans.

Bay kou blié, poté mak sôjé.
He who strikes the blow forgets,
he who bears the marks remembers.

Early morningsongs in the streets of New Orleans rejoice in sad-glad lyrics and vibrant outcries resonating from the souls of the descendants of African ancestors. Silence awakes to the singing voices of vendors in three-part harmony: "It's yo' Ve-gi-teh-ble Man . . . ah got Irish potatoes, sweet po-ta-toes, fresh swimp an' toe-may-toes, laaaaaay-dy!" Barking dogs announce the arrival of an old mule-drawn wagon. A large rusty cowbell hung loosely around the mule's neck sways unhurriedly, ringing CA-LANK CA-CLANG with every step. "Rag man . . . Rag man!" shouts the person seated high on the front of the wagon. Like a work of abstract expressionism, old clothes, rags, and cloth lie disheveled in a mosaic of colors in the back of the wagon. "Woe, Mule," commands the Rag Man as the wagon stops to receive an armload of used clothing, "Up-in-nare mule," intones the Rag Man. His proud voice—like a slow blues song contemplating the few dollars this day may bring—refuses to allow poverty to crush his resilient spirit.

The morning air is punctuated with the warm greetings of friends: "Hey, bey-bey! How you makin' it? . . . For true?" Silence struggles for survival in a city that enjoys life. On any given day, the unknown becomes known in the streets as polyrhythmic sounds of parades with their funky jazz brass give music to dancing feet.

Celebration seems to come easy in New Orleans. Perhaps it is one reason the city is called "the Big Easy," "the city that care forgot"! Relaxed intensity prevails over moods of impatience. "Things" get done not in the cold impersonal ways of

New York City, but in ways best described as interpersonal caring. It is a response similar to the Brazilian *jeito*—another way of doing things, of finding solutions to seemingly insurmountable problems, of meeting an impasse with compassion. Self-discipline is subtle, as if the thresholds of acceptable behavior are clear in the minds of the people. Conflicts are most often resolved in a compromise of verbal laughter: "Yeah, you right!" Moral boundaries are left to religious leaders, who make the most of celebrations such as weddings to reach those who miss the Sunday sermons. As one Baptist minister told his small congregation of African-Americans: "Know your limits . . . even Christ couldn't take a fourth nail!"

Seaport cities are filled with the cumulative wisdom of ages: of the comings and goings of buyers and sellers, of truthful liars and lying truths, of traders and salesmen bent on making profits at the expense of human dignity. New Orleans is one of those cities along a mighty river, the Mississippi, that has witnessed a history in North America like no other. It is a history filled with contrasts, extremes that tested the limits of the fourth nail. Like many riverbank civilizations, New Orleans endured its pain and resurrected its pleasures to provide the world with unique cultural expressions. The roots of those expressions were nurtured in the rich black soil of African cultures transplanted to the swampy lands of early New Orleans. The horrors of slavery brought Africans—*Nègres*—to rescue New Orleans from its own corruption, from its failure to sustain itself as a French colony, and from a destiny of self-destruction. It was upon the backs of enslaved Africans and their descendants that New Orleans was built to become the second largest seaport in the United States.

Africans first came to Louisiana in great numbers in 1719 aboard French slave ships from Senegambia, the region along the west coast of Africa between Senegal and

Gambia. In 1709, however, several enslaved Africans had already been smuggled there from Havana by Jean Baptist Le Moyne Bienville. In *Africans in Colonial Louisiana*, a definitive study based on slave-ship documents and court records, Gwendolyn Midlo Hall concludes that in the ten-year period 1720-1730 nearly all the slaves were brought to Louisiana directly from Africa. Hall states that two thirds of the slaves came from Senegambia, the rest from the Bight of Benin (Nigeria), the Congo, and Angola.

Native Americans, or AmerIndians, had lived along the Mississippi River before the French colonizers arrived. They were the "first people," primal—not primitive—people. Like Africans along the Senegal River who shared a common language, neighboring AmerIndians communicated in a language that most tribes understood. Along the rich farmlands of the Mississippi River valley, communities such as the Natchez, Chawasha, Bayogoula, Houma, and Quinipissa belonged to the same linguistic family known as Muskhogean. AmerIndians had developed a complex civilization. They possessed a strong sense of spirituality, and their sacred beliefs were reflected in songs and religious rituals. They wore costumes and feather crowns "embellished with little beads or small white seeds as hard as beads."

Africans and AmerIndians in Louisiana had more in common than they had differences. Their lifestyles were shaped by a basic need for survival along rivers. They knew how to live in harmony with nature, how to avoid starvation—the principal enemy of the European colonizers. With the first arrival of the French, the AmerIndians were friendly and helpful. Later, it became obvious that the French wanted to control the territory, to claim huge tracts of fertile lands occupied by AmerIndians. The French tried to enslave the AmerIndians, but were not very successful. As soon as an opportunity presented itself, the AmerIndian slave would escape, often taking enslaved

Africans with him. They discovered mutual likes and dislikes, a value base forged by spiritual beliefs—an *élan vital*—music and drum rhythms, the use of herbs in healing and spices such as *filé* in the preparation of foods, and a knowledge of farming technology that produced bountiful harvests of corn, rice, okra, and other crops. A common bond was established between two oppressed peoples in Louisiana: Africans and AmerIndians.

Resistance to slavery and French colonization by Native Americans and Africans escalated into uprisings and wars. The Natchez fought three fierce wars against the French in 1716, 1722, and 1729. Many enslaved Africans who escaped were given refuge by the Native Americans, and joined in wars against the French.

In the war of 1729, the Natchez were winning. In desperation, the French persuaded a sizable group of Choctaw to help them fight, and with their help the French were able to defeat the Natchez, forcing them to leave their lands. In 1731, an estimated 450 Natchez were captured and sold into slavery in Santo Domingo (Haiti), which had also been colonized by the French. The remaining Natchez refugees relocated far and wide, living with the Creek, Cherokee, and other communities. The might of the French cannon along with imported diseases such as smallpox decimated the AmerIndian population along the Mississippi.

In 1718, the year of the official founding of New Orleans, Bienville was appointed colonial governor of Louisiana. The white population of Louisiana decreased from 5,400 in 1721 to 1,700 by 1724, while the African population increased to 3,500. Fear of uprisings by African slaves on the plantations and in the colony prompted Governor Bienville in 1724 to enact the Code Noir or Black Code.

The first article of the code ordered the expulsion of all Jews from the colony. The succeeding four articles prohibited all forms of worship except Roman Catholic, required masters to give religious instruction to their slaves, and provided for the confiscation of blacks who were supervised by non-Catholics or found at work on Sundays or holy days. The Black Code prohibited concubinage and marriage of both whites and freeborn or freed blacks with slaves. Article 6 stated: "We forbid our white subjects, of both sexes, to marry with the Blacks under the penalty of being fined or subjected to some other arbitrary punishment." But, as one historian observed, "Propinquity and personality were more than a match for prejudice." In the heat of the night many babies were conceived of mixed blood, known today as Creoles, *Gens de Couleur.*

In 1803, General Napoleon Bonaparte, in need of money to finance his war efforts, sold Louisiana to the United States for $15,000,000, less than four cents an acre. The area of the Louisiana Purchase was subdivided by an act of Congress into the Missouri Territory and the Territory of Orleans. The Census of 1803 lists a population in Louisiana of 42,000, more than half of whom were African slaves and Creoles. Seven years later, in 1810, the aggregate population was 76,556, of whom 34,311 were whites, 7,585 were Creoles, and 34,660 were enslaved Africans. Now under American rule, Louisiana in 1812 adopted a constitution that deprived Creoles of many of the few rights they had enjoyed under French and Spanish rule. Disenfranchised by fearful planters, merchants, and newly arrived "Yankees" who had moved South, they found themselves citizens without citizenship.

Incredibly, at the outbreak of the Civil War, Southern whites turned to Creoles and *Nègres* to help them defend "Southern rights." Many did fight, reluctantly, on the side of the Confederacy. But the majority of Creole and African-American soldiers, numbering some 15,000, fought in the Union Army in four Colored regiments under the command of General Benjamin F. Butler. Louisiana, occupied by Union troops, abolished slavery through the Reconstruction Constitution of 1864. By the close of the Civil War on April 9, 1865, 80,000 blacks had been killed.

On September 27, 1865, the then liberal Republican Party of Louisiana, headed by twenty-six members, five of whom were blacks, called a convention in New Orleans. They denounced the debasement of the rights guaranteed by the federal Constitution and demanded "liberty and equality of all men before the law." They elected Henry Clay Warmuth to present their recommendations to Congress.

The Louisiana Democratic Party, a conservative group of nineteenth-century Southern politicians, also assembled a state convention in New Orleans. On October 2, 1865 they declared: " . . . this is to be a Government of White People, made and to be perpetuated for the exclusive political benefit of the White Race, and . . . the people of African descent cannot be considered as citizens of the United States, and there can in no event nor under any circumstances be any equality between the White and other Races."

Despite this dissidence, the Thirteenth Amendment to the Constitution was ratified on December 18, 1865, abolishing slavery forever in the United States. However, rights of citizenship and "equal protection" under the law did not become law until the following year with the ratification of the Fourteenth and Fifteenth Amendments. African-Americans finally began to taste the fruits of equality. During the period of Reconstruction (1865-1877), many African-Americans were elected to public office. In Louisiana, the state government was in the hands of seven officers, two of whom were African-Americans. The Louisiana state legislature added an amendment abolishing slavery to the Reconstruction Constitution and provided that no public schools or other educational institutions should exist for the exclusive use of one race. They also enacted the first public accommodations law, providing that all places of business or public entertainment should be open to all without regard to race or color.

Hostile reaction among whites took the form of clandestine terrorism and open mob violence, originating principally from white racist groups such as the Ku Klux Klan, the Knights of the White Camellia, and the Innocents. On September 14, 1874, five thousand Knights of the White Camellia, armed with rifles and shotguns, seized control of New Orleans. Thirty-two persons were killed and seventy wounded before federal troops quelled the rebellion on orders from President Ulysses S. Grant.

Federal troops remained in Louisiana until 1877, when President Rutherford B. Hayes ordered their removal. In doing so, he removed a protective safeguard of the rights of people of African descent guaranteed by the Constitution. In 1896, the US Supreme Court, in the famous *Plessy* v. *Ferguson* decision of "separate but equal," mandated segregation of whites and blacks throughout the United States.

The Louisiana Constitutional Convention met in New Orleans on February 8, 1898, to draft a new constitution to replace the Reconstruction Constitution imposed by the Union. They created a "White Supremacy Constitution." Among the acts established in the new constitution against persons of African descent were: (1) the "Understanding Clause": to qualify for voter registration the citizen had to interpret the Constitution; (2) the "Grandfather Clause," which exempted any male of at least twenty-one years of age from the educational and property requirements needed to register to vote, provided his father or grandfather had the right to vote before January 1, 1867, which enslaved Africans and Creoles had not; (3) the refusal to register anyone without a receipt showing the annual payment of a $1 poll tax; and (4) other nebulous "voter qualifications."

Joanne Grant comments on this situation in *Black Protest: History, Documents, and Analyses, 1619 to the Present*:

> In Louisiana in 1896, there were 164,088 whites registered and 130,344 Negroes. In 1900, the first registration year after a new constitution had been adopted, there were 125,437 whites and 5,320 Negroes registered. By 1904, Negro registration had declined to 1,718, and white registration was 106,360. This represented a 96% decrease in Negro registration, and a 4% decrease in white.

It was during this period of disenfranchisement near the turn of the century that the resilient spirit of Africans in the United States awakened and exploded in original expressions of aesthetic value. In New Orleans, two profound manifestations were born: jazz music and the Mardi Gras celebrations of the Black Indians. One of the first creators of jazz was African-American trumpeter Buddy Bolden in the 1890s. The rest is history! New Orleans has given to the world a form of music that is truly "American," a music created by people of African descent. Little known, however, is another response, commonly called the "Mardi Gras Indians," persons of African and AmerIndian descent who hold an alternative Mardi Gras celebration in the backstreets of New Orleans. Their one-of-a-kind original costumes celebrate the culture and heritage of the AmerIndians, with whom their African ancestors lived in freedom, fought, and intermarried.

Imagine awakening at dawn on Mardi Gras to the sound of tambourines and singing in the streets. You look cautiously out the window to see a group of black men dancing down the street in colorful, bejeweled AmerIndian-style costumes. "Oooo-Na-Nah...Git out dee way" sings the Spyboy, the scout, who is the first member to be seen. He carries a shotgun wrapped in pink cloth, the color of his costume. The cloth is decorated with large semiprecious stones circled with rhinestones, each sewn

Big Chief Gerald "Jake" Millon and son of the White Eagles tribe.

meticulously by hand. He pauses at the corner, whirls around in a crouching motion, and suddenly leaps in the air, turning to face those who follow. *"Coo-chee mali!"* he yells, "Spyyyy-boy...*Coo-chee mali*, bahmmm-bahmmm!" He fires a shot into the air and opens his arms to signal that "all is clear."

Marching in single file through the black neighborhoods of New Orleans are the Black Indians of Mardi Gras. They are spaced at intervals of several yards or as much as a city block between costumed members. Next in the line of march is the Flagboy, carrying a banner on a metal rod. His costume is bright yellow, embellished with hundreds of rhinestones. He is followed by the Gang Flag, another flagboy, in a red costume that seems to change shades as he moves in and out of the early-morning sun. He holds a staff ten to twelve feet long, covered with designs in looping patterns, trimmed in marabou, and topped with long plumes or feathers. Somewhere on this sculptured staff are the initials of his tribe in large gemstones such as Y.P. for Yellow Pocahontas, W.E. for White Eagles, or W.T. for Wild Tchoupitoulas. There are nearly two dozen Black Indian "gangs" or tribes in New Orleans.

Seemingly out of nowhere the Wild Man appears. His costume color is brown, with patches of animal fur accentuating an intricately beaded apron. Protruding from the top of his crown are two cow horns. He leaps around in a frenzy and is known to knock down fences, garbage cans, or anything in his way. The Wild Man runs back to the Third Chief and dances around him; the Chief, dressed in blue, smiles approval. He is followed by the Second Chief, who is accompanied by a woman in costume known as a Queen. Both wear magnificent costumes of brilliant orange. At the end of the line of march is the Big Chief, his white costume the finest of all, with a huge crown adorned with beads and rhinestones.

Hundreds of non-costumed African-Americans follow

the Black Indians, singing and playing tambourines, wood blocks, a wine-bottle-hit-with-a-comb, an empty antifreeze container that is now a small yellow drum, a bass drum, smaller drums, and various other percussive instruments. This chorus, called the Second Line, chants in call-and-response patterns. The lead singer is heard above the crowd: "Oh, the Golden Crown, the Golden Crown" and the chorus responds: "Big Chief Tootie got the Golden Crown" (Lead singer): "Big Chief Tootie's gonna take em' down" (Chorus): "Big Chief Tootie got the Golden Crown!"

They continue through the back streets of New Orleans until they meet another tribe. In the old days when two tribes met they would fight. They carried pistols, knives, and razor-sharp hatchets. If one chief refused to "Humbah" (bow humbly to the other chief), a shootout would ensue. Today, bloody violence has stopped. "They try to out-dress one another," says Big Chief Allison "Tootie" Montana of the Yellow Pocahontas tribe. "When they meet me on Carnival Day, I put the hurt on 'em. I'm so pretty that they all have to come up and shake my hand and say: 'Chief, I've got to give it to you. You did it again!'"

Big Chief "Tootie" designs his original costume in three-dimensional abstract patterns. His huge crown encircles his head and body and contains more than 350 feathers. According to tradition, the costume is worn only twice: on Mardi Gras, "Fat Tuesday," the day before the beginning of Lent in the Roman Catholic religion; and on the Feast of St. Joseph a few weeks later. This has now been replaced by two "Super Sunday" parades, when tribes uptown and downtown march together.

After the costumes are worn, they are dismantled and destroyed. A new costume must be created for the following year. Months of preparation go into the making of a "suit." It is a communal effort. Men and women sit around in the evenings sewing beads and stones on "patches" that will later be put into the suit. Each patch tells a story and must fit into the closely guarded secret—the dominant color of that year's costume.

There are two principal styles of costumes, the "Uptown Indians" and the "Downtown Indians." The Uptown Indians use beads and stones in a two dimensional motif to make a theme sketched on canvas come alive. Usually, animals are depicted on the costumes and must be consistent throughout the suit. Respect for AmerIndians is often the theme expressed in beads. Faces of AmerIndian Chiefs, warriors, scenes of AmerIndians at work, at play, or engaged in a conflict are also depicted. The Downtown Indians create three dimensional abstract patterns throughout the costumes. The crown, reminiscent of a warbonnet, is the most prized possession. The diadem is beaded and embellished with large semi-precious stones. The Uptown Indians use plumes in their crowns, while the Downtown Indians adhere to the more traditional use of feathers.

This cultural manifestation in New Orleans originated in the 1880s. A group of black men appeared on Carnival day dressed as AmerIndians. They called themselves the "Creole Wild West." Their first chief was Becate Batiste, of African and AmerIndian descent, the great-uncle of Big Chief "Tootie" Montana. The tradition was handed down from father to son in the Montana family. It has evolved as a living cradle of African and AmerIndian culture.

A closer look at the lyrics of the Black Indians' songs gives clues to how the people felt about their life and the forces that surrounded them. They have a variety of songs that are sung in call-and-response patterns. Every Sunday evening after church, months before Carnival, they meet at a "practice." Here in the back room of a neighborhood bar, one finds the best singing and polyrhythmic accompaniment. There are songs of boastful joy: "My Big Chief got da Golden Crown"; songs of courage: "Corey died on the

Battlefield" (Corey was a Spyboy ambushed by a hostile tribe who fought to his death); songs of hope (for good weather): "Shallow Water Lil' Mama!"; songs of lament when someone dies: "Brother Herc is Gone" or "Brother John is Gone" and "We Love Our President" (sung at the death of President Kennedy); and dancing songs: "Lil' Liza Jane" and *"Tu Es Pas Ka-Way"* (pronounced "two-way pocka-way.").

Embedded in the song lyrics are retentions from African languages and expressions brought across on slave ships. For example, when a Big Chief emerges from his house on Mardi Gras he sings the "Indian Prayer Song": *"Mah-day, cootie fiyo"*; and the crowd responds, "Indian red, Indian-un raid!" The Big Chief sings: "Now look at my Spyboy, Spyboy: a wild, wild creation, the best in the nation . . . and he won't bow down, no he won't bow down, on that dirty ground, because I love to hear him call My Indian Red!"

In the long history of oppression in Louisiana, AmerIndians and blacks helped one another in a common effort to maintain their culture, language, and sacred beliefs. Persons of African descent in New Orleans have an innate respect for the resistance of AmerIndians to colonization and discrimination.

The impact of the Mardi Gras Indians and the respect for their cultural expression is summed up in the film documentary "The Black Indians of New Orleans." Oral historian Abe Sturgis says: ". . . the Mardi Gras Indian is something that you just got to be part of, the feeling of what it's all about. Everything we do in this city regardless of what we play, whether they call it 'Jazz' or 'Soul' or 'Gospel' or whatever you call it, it all has TWO-WAY POCKA-WAY in it. It's something about our music, they all have that 1-2-3-4, DUN-TA-DUN-DUNT, you know, that's always in there. It's just part of the natural rhythm that went all the way back to the Marie Laveau thing, and the voodoo things that was going on in Congo Square years ago. It's just part of our heritage. You can be sitting down, and the tambourines start ringing . . . . some people call it 'Funk', but you know it's strictly us, it's 'Second Line.' It's something to get your blood warmed up and make your feet begin to move, and you start being part of your self, the real you. And the beautiful part about it is that no two people can express themselves the same way. Everyone is feeling what they feel, and it's all basically a proud thing, and it's a happy thing; it's a sad thing. It's a joyous thing . . . it's all these things combined!"

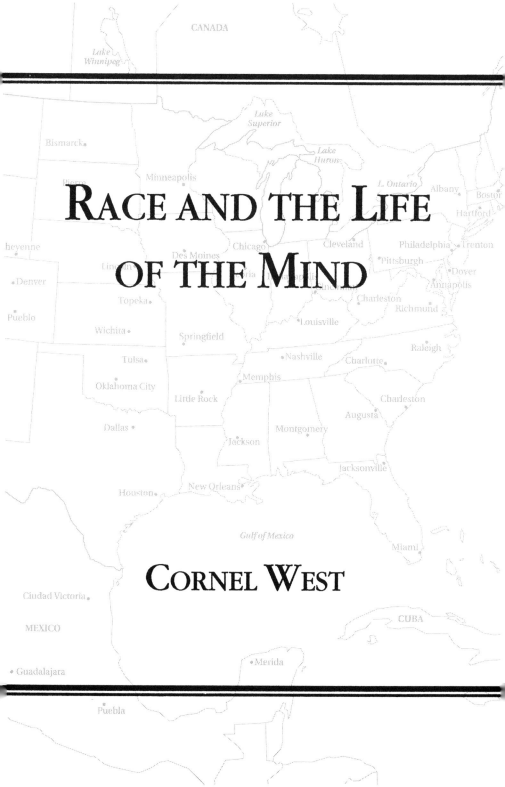

RACE AND THE LIFE OF THE MIND

CORNEL WEST

© Benno Friedman

Cornel West was born in Tulsa, Oklahoma. He holds a master's degree and PhD from Princeton University.

Professor West is the author of numerous books, including *Prophetic Fragments, Race Matters,* and most recently, *Keeping Faith.* His essays have appeared in a number of other journals and other publications.

Professor West lectures extensively at universities and at religious and civic organizations. He has been a guest lecturer and visiting scholar at many universities and was recently W. E. B. Du Bois Lecturer at Harvard University. Professor West is currently a professor of religion and director of the Afro-American Studies Department at Princeton University.

Professor West lives in Princeton with his wife, Elleni, and son, Clifton. He is currently working with coauthor Michael Lerner on the forthcoming book *Blacks and Jews: Conflicts and Coalescence.*

The following selection is adapted from a speech delivered by Professor West in October 1993.

Ⅰt is an inspiration to believe that through the life of the mind
we as citizens can cultivate the critical sensibilities we know
to be requisite for creating and sustaining a vibrant public life.
A vibrant public life is a precondition and prerequisite of a
vital democracy, as John Dewey wrote in 1927.

I come at this idea not so much as an individual as from
within the framework of a tradition. That tradition has as
much to do with John Dewey as it does with W. E. B. Du
Bois and a host of others—the tradition of struggle. I
decided many years ago that I would give my time and
energy and if need be my life for this particular tradition. I
take quite seriously the powerful formulation of T. S. Eliot
in his essay of 1919, "Tradition and the Individual Talent":
"[Tradition] cannot be inherited, and if you want it you
must obtain it by great labour." His conceptual tradition is
different from mine in tone and content and substance,
needless to say. But he's absolutely right about the rules,
the plight, and the labor—the intellectual and existential
and personal labor—necessary if one is to transmit the
best tradition. The tradition I'm talking about is a radical
democratic tradition. This tradition is rooted in the notion
that ordinary people ought to live lives of decency and
dignity. And therefore ordinary people ought to be able to
have a significant say at the highest levels of decision-
making in those institutions that guide and regulate their
lives. This is the tradition that in the seventeenth century
made Blaise Pascal have faith in ordinary people and
believe that Promethean energies exist everywhere, energies that, unleashed, can produce possibilities heretofore
downplayed, ignored, overlooked.

For me, democracy does not belong only in government.
It is not simply a way in which human beings ought to
interact in order to mediate their various conflicts and

147

cleavages. It is a mode of being in the world. The same can be said of jazz. Jazz is not just an art form; it is deeper. It is a democratic mode of being in the world in which mutual respect, enablement, empowerment, openness, criticism and self-criticism, correction and self-correction sit at the very center of any particular enterprise of which one is a part. In a jazz quartet, leaders like Duke Ellington or Count Basie participate in an improvisational and disciplined fashion. This means much for a citizen who tries to apply the life of the mind to public affairs in a democratic society.

Why? Because I think historian Richard Hofstadter was right. In his great text of 1963, *Anti-Intellectualism in American Life*, he drew a distinction between intellect and intelligence. You know many highly intelligent people who are not intellectuals. Intelligence is about manipulation and readjustment. Intellect is about wonder, curiosity. Not just evaluating, but evaluating evaluations, discerning tacit assumptions and unarticulated presuppositions, not just dealing with the questions, but trying to keep in touch with the larger framework in which the questions are asked. That's what intellectuals are about. It is that kind of critical thinking that sustains a vital democracy.

A certain piety goes with intellect that has very little to do with religion in the common sense of the term. This piety has to do with a sense of calling, of vocation, a sense of following through on the argument and of following the evidence where it leads. At its best it is emancipatory, liberatory.

The tradition I mentioned before, the radical democratic tradition, was introduced to me by the Black Freedom Movement. I come out of a particular experience in which white supremacists bombarded black beauty, black intelligence, black capacity, black capability—oh yes, and black humanity. And in the face of those assaults and attacks were forged various conceptions of identity and community and loyalty and love and care and concern: black love, black care, black concern. For me, the Black Freedom Movement is a species emerging from the radical democratic tradition.

I believe that the radical democratic tradition is the best tradition that we human beings have been able to forge since the beginning of civilization—we linguistically deeply conscious creatures, born between urine and feces, who weave webs of meaning and significance even as we know we face inescapable extinction of some sort. That is why for me the radical democratic tradition is so precious: The Black Freedom Movement at its best, and other movements of this same tradition, highlight the dignity, the sense of the tragic, the sublime grandeur of everyday people, ordinary people.

This same tradition led to my experiences at Harvard and at Princeton. For me Harvard and Princeton were empowering experiences, emancipating and liberating even as they had their own provincialisms and parochialisms. I would move from one kind of parochialism to another but still have liberating moments, expansion of horizons, and, most important for me, a sense of empowerment, intellectually, existentially, personally, ethically, and politically. A sense of empowerment: being able to feel as if life is a kind of adventure, as if life is exploration.

In reflecting on race and its impact on the life of the mind, I want first to cite four distinctive features that I think must exist for a serious discussion of race. I believe that these features actually pertain to any issue at all.

First and foremost is a sense of history. A nuanced sense of history, a subtle sense of history. I think we have to admit the degree to which a sense of history is deeply un-American. Henry Ford spoke for many Americans when he said, "History is bunk." America is all about the past at our back, as Emerson suggests. For Americans everything good is on the highway, Emerson writes in "Circles." It's Huck on the boat, it's Ahab on the ship, Kerouac *On the Road*. It's so American: mobility, individuality, limply holding on to traditions—history, society. Don't dock your boat for long, keep moving.

But we know there's history on that boat. There are power relations on that boat, contestation on that boat, friendship on that boat. You can't escape history. How difficult is what Henry James called a "hotel civilization." That's how he described America from England. What did he mean by a hotel civilization? What is a hotel? A fusion of market and home. Isn't that so American! We want the warmth, the security of the home, that haven in a heartless world. But we love the market. Competitive, rugged, ragged with rapacious individualism, the liquidity, the materiality of that market, always moving. The fluidity and flexibility of that market.

But both home and the market are deeply private phenomena. Neither is concerned about common good, public interest, interaction of persons across communities, across enclaves, be they ethnic, racial, or what have you. Henry James was on to something deep about Americans' difficulty in having a sense of history.

You can't talk about race in America without a sense of history. Often in contemporary discussion, as soon as you bring up history people say, "Oh, my God, here comes the wallowing in self-pity, here come the guilt buttons to be pushed." But the tragic facts of the past shape the present. Eliot called it the pastness of the present. He is right. It ought not to suffocate us. It ought not to disenable us to acknowledge a great tradition. Any debate in the present is shaped by various interpretations of the past.

But it has to be a nuanced sense of history. Often when Americans talk about a sense of history, it is cast in melodramatic Manichean terms: all the good on one side, all the bad on the other. History is about ambiguous legacies. There are no pure and pristine cultures, but hybrid cultures. Civilizations ebbed and flowed, rising and falling. That's why I find it useful to remind my students what

Hegel called history: a slaughterhouse in which blood flows.

I'm calling not for a melodramatic conception of history, but for a tragic sense of history, a Melville or a Faulkner, a Toni Morrison, in which existential bruises and psychic scars and ontological wounds, heartbreaks and heartaches, sadness and sorrow, serve as backdrop for human action and human agency. That is what the tragic is about.

A tragic sense of history links us to a sense of the subtle and the nuanced. When we talk about race we are not talking about relations between typecast persons, any more than we live in homogeneous towns. There is no such thing as "white people" or "black people." Part of white supremacist discourse is precisely the intent to cast groups in monolithic and homogeneous ways. Isn't that what Ralph Ellison was all about in *Invisible Man* in 1952: human visibility? White supremacist discourse has claimed that black people form one homogeneous blob in which each and every black person is interchangeable and substitutable, so you only need one black leader because all black people think the same way. I used to experience this sometimes at Harvard. Any time the issue of race would arise, they would all look at me, "Would you please say now on behalf of thirty million black folks what you think about the race issue?" No, but I'll tell you my sense of history. I believe in diversity and multiplicity and heterogeneity in the black community just as I believe in diversity and multiplicity and heterogeneity in the white community. I'm not going to lose sight of Elijah Lovejoy shot on his roof in Alton, Illinois, in 1837 as part of the Black Freedom Movement. I'm not going to lose sight of Rosa Parks or Lydia Maria Child, who would write that powerful text in 1833, "An Appeal in Favor of That Class of Americans Called Africans." There is heterogeneity among white folk, too, but white supremacy is still denying it or overlooking it. A nuanced sense of history would

151

allow for a certain kind of openness in the dialogue, opening us to be self-critical.

A nuanced sense of history goes hand in hand with a subtle social analysis. To talk about history, of course, is not to talk about history in the abstract. It is to talk about the operations of wealth and power and status and prestige. To talk about race in the United States is, for me, to talk about poor people. The problem in the black community has been twofold: too much poverty and too little self-love. Too much black poverty means too much poverty in the country, in the world. Looking to the life of the mind might mean choosing directional tools that would generate insight as to why it is that we live in the richest nation in the history of the world but there is still so much poverty. Even in 1993, 1 percent of the population owned 48 percent of the financial net wealth. I call that oligarchy, I call that plutocracy. A deep nuanced historical sense would provide us with some means of trying to account for the various ways in which democracy itself, grand and precious as it ideally is, has been truncated, limited, constrained, as it were.

In 1776 white men without property couldn't vote. Jacksonian democracy: white men with property can vote. As conquest of indigenous peoples escalates in the nineteenth century, the tightening of chains increases. August 1920: The majority of Americans finally can vote—women. In 1964* twelfth-generation Americans like my grandmother can finally vote—in a country that is overwhelmingly less than third-generation American. Truncated democracy: precious ideal, limited practice. A nuanced sense of history links an analysis of wealth and power.

---

*The 1964 Civil Rights Act was the most far-reaching civil rights bill since the Reconstruction era. Among other provisions, it helped guarantee the right of African-Americans to vote and to have full access to public accommodations and employment opportunities. The 1965 Voter Rights Act later fully guaranteed voting rights to African-American voters.

A nuanced sense of history and subtle analysis of power and wealth play a very important role. But in addition to these we need a second feature, something that's going out of fashion: an all-embracing moral vision.

We live in a time when the ideology of the century is nationalism. There's a host of forms of xenophobia at our feet—in Bosnia, South Africa. We cut against the grain by projecting an all-embracing moral vision in which we not only commit ourselves to the life of the mind but insist on being concerned about the degree to which creatures are responding to circumstances—circumstances in which they are born, not of their own choosing. The link between historical consciousness and empathy for other human beings was cast so well by Simone Weil, the great French Christophilic philosopher. She said that love of thy neighbor in all its fullness means being able to say to him or her, "What are you going through?"

Keep track of historical circumstances. You can get a sense of the frustrations and anxieties of other people. You can put yourself in their place and in their shoes. John Howard Griffin's book of 1962, *Black Like Me*, had a tremendous impact. It was written by one white American who had no sense of what it was like to be in black skin. Granted, he didn't stay there too long; in the last chapter he was glad to get out of that black body. But John Howard Griffin had a point. He said, I want to empathize in such a way that I shall experience the circumstances. It won't be an abstract relationship mediated by pity. It will be a concrete one mediated by empathy. An all-embracing moral vision is all about that sort of love and sympathy and empathy. It ought to be linked to a subtle sense of history so that one has a sense of what people are up against, *whoever they are.*

But an all-embracing moral vision is going out of fashion because we live in such a balkanized and pulverized and divided society. America is the most segregated society in

153

housing patterns with the exception of South Africa. An overwhelming majority of white persons who live in vanilla suburbs live in suburbs that are less than 1 percent black. And then we raise the question, "Why are our children always having problems acquiring the skill of interacting with other folk?" Where did they grow up? Their heroes are black, by means of vicarious experiments in colorvision: Arsenio, Oprah, Michael Jackson, Michael Jordan, Prince. But for flesh-and-blood black bodies, where does the interaction—especially the humane interaction—take place in such a de facto segregated society? How do you generate the possibilities of empathy and sympathy, given such fragmentation of living space? These are questions with which we have to deal. Many of our white students come to us, hungry, thirsty to learn about this other set of American experiences—of indigenous peoples and black peoples and brown peoples— feeling unable to bridge that divide. And it's not just a matter of rubbing up against their intellectuals. Read *Black Boy*. Read *Native Son* and try to get inside of Bigger's mind. Deal with that fury and that anger. Then you'll understand a little bit of what "Public Enemy" is all about: black rage. The sense of having one's back against the wall, then responding in a variety of ways. Empathy is inextricably linked to a deep, tragic sense of history.

Third, there's a need for self-critical courageous stances. By that I mean that particular emancipatory moment in one's own experience in which one recognizes the truth of Nietzsche's comment that it's often not simply a matter of having the courage of one's convictions, but also having the courage to attack one's convictions. It's another way of putting Socrates' simple formulation that the unexamined life is not worth living, but also acknowledging that the examined life is painful, full of risk and vulnerability. It is pushing oneself to the edge of life's abyss, as it were, and recognizing that maturity, development, and growth can take place by feeling that what was once a foundation is pudding-like.

In typical American fashion, our great philosopher Charles Sanders Peirce put it differently. He said, "Do not block the way of inquiry." And we will add, "Any travelers who have the courage to engage in conversation linked to high-quality inquiry must be willing to put their power and relative ignorance under the spotlight."

That's dangerous, very dangerous. Because anybody who enters has to say, "Here is my cultural baggage, here are my presuppositions, here are my prejudices, here are my pre-judgments. Let's put the spotlight onto them and see whether in fact they can be sustained. Here are my silences, here are my blindnesses. Bring them to light." That is a self-critical courageous stance. That is why it is so very difficult.

Look at Malcolm X. Fragile identity. Growing up on the streets of Omaha, Lansing, Harlem, trying to find himself, echoing that sentence in *The Souls of Black Folk*, when Du Bois was talking about Alexander Cronin, "This is a history of a human heart,—the tale of a black boy who many years ago began to struggle with life that he might know the world and know himself." Malcolm X finally gained some sense of himself in that cell in Norfolk State Prison in Massachusetts and had the courage to do what very few of us have: to attack his most precious conviction, the very conviction that held him together, given his fragile identity, given his difficult childhood and the white supremacy coming at him. He gave that self-critique in 1964. He was growing because he wanted to grow, he was determined. What a grand example.

The fourth feature is the sense of audacious hope. Those who have a nuanced sense of history, a subtle social analysis, an all-embracing moral vision, and a self-critical courageous stance ought to have what Rabbi Abraham Joshua Heschel called radical amazement and what I call audacious hope, as opposed to optimism. I think optimism is too much a notion of being able to move and act based solely upon the evidence. That notion was beautifully demystified by William James in his essay, "The Sentiment of Rationality." It gave him a structure of faith and clarified in what way talk about hope is different from talk about optimism. James was not casting it in any religious formulation or particular tradition. He was talking about human beings who have to look at evidence that is underdetermined and who must still make leaps of faith, because doubt is always possible, because one can always question any attempt to do something that looks impossible. Audacious hope: energizing and galvanizing persons, convincing persons to get fired up even in the face of a civilization that we all know to be in deep decline and decay.

Now, what does it mean to talk about the present as history shaped by the past, but also very different from the past? I suggest in *Race Matters* that we live in a time in which there is an unprecedented lethal linkage between economic decline, cultural decay, and political malaise. I'm not going to say a word about economic decline and political malaise.

But I am going to talk about cultural decay. By cultural decay I mean the promotion of spiritual impoverishment by a market culture that promotes the notion that we are viable and vibrant only when we are addicted and stimulated. That addiction and stimulation revolve around buying, selling, promoting, and advertising. They focus primarily on sexual foreplay and orgiastic intensity, often in the form of degrading women. We are stimulated in a base, bodily way. It's a market culture. Very different from what Adam Smith had in mind. Smith knew that a market economy could not be predicated on a market culture. In the same way, that basic symbol of a market economy, namely, the contract, must presuppose noncontractual values. Contracts mean nothing in a culture in which promise-keeping and truth-telling mean nothing.

Market culture is not something new. Its intensity has always been here, but the pace has increased. Young people today are creatures of a market culture like no other generation in the history of the world. It was very different when I was growing up. Then we still had at least spaces for nonmarket values in a market culture: family, neighborhood, buildings, dance companies, apprenticeship networks, and music. Athletics was a male-bonding activity in those days; I know it's been democratized since. Nonmarket values—like love and care and concern; and even in our personal relationships, tenderness, kindness, gentleness—remember those? Now it's all about performance, about bodies stimulating each other, about manipulation, subordination, domination. Why? It's because market values are now fundamentally socializing and acculturating young people, which makes it very difficult for emotional bonds and supportive networks to have weight and gravity in their lives. It's leaving our youth rootless and culturally denuded, like oranges without a peel, having to deal with what human beings have always had to deal with, death and disease and despair and dread, but now with very little armor. Without the love and care and concern, how do you deal with these? Without narratives and stories and legends and rituals, how do you deal with these? Overwhelmed by the market forces, Americans are looking for what Pascal called diversion. Down and out? Go to the mall. Isn't that the last of the public spaces around? Dedicated to what? Buying and selling. Feeling gloomy? Turn on the television and engage in that spectatorial passivity in which you're bombarded to be stimulated. None of us escapes.

This is what we're up against. How does one make the life of the mind attractive in this context? Is it possible any longer to cultivate the critical sensibilities requisite for a vital democracy in such a culture? Nonmarket values in

America—justice, community, freedom, love—cut against the grain. Commitment to the life of the mind means taking non-market values seriously to such a degree that we call into question the assumptions upon which cultures, economies, and societies rest. Those who take the life of the mind seriously are, in fact, transgressive, maybe even subversive.

Then what are we to do? I think we ought to regenerate public life. We regenerate public life by trying to learn once again the art of public conversation. Because in a civilization such as ours most public conversation consists of name-calling, the clashing of identities and constituencies, and various melodramatic versions of history. But public-mindedness is crucial for public life. Either public conversation must be regenerated and rejuvenated or we all slide down a slippery slope of cocoon-like privatism.

We live in one of the most frightening and terrible moments in the history of this country, but we do have a chance to create a window of opportunity in which we once again extend the public conversation. We can only do it by confronting our history in a nuanced and subtle way, by acknowledging the role of wealth and power, trying to be self-critical in a humble way—intellectual humility here being crucial—while taking a stance and holding on to a sense of hope. As Du Bois put it when he was looking at the riots in Atlanta, tears in his eyes: We must do something. We've got to keep fighting, no matter how bad and difficult things are.

We are part of this conversation, this dialogue with these figures of old and the present. They're pointing to something bigger than us, which is humbling but empowering, luring the best and critical of the worst in us. That is a difficult challenge. As it was once put it so well: If we can acknowledge that it is always dawn, that somewhere above the eastern horizon the sun is now on the people, there's possibility. Let's see whether we can seize it. It's up to us.

Glossary

abolitionist—one who favors elimination of a practice or institution, especially of Negro slavery in the US

abomination—something abhorred or loathed

accoutrement—equipment or trappings

acculturate—adapt to a different culture

acrid—bitterly pungent, irritating, corrosive in temper or manner

adorn—add beauty or luster to

aesthetic—concerned with beauty or the appreciation of beauty; ideal of beauty

anoint—apply oil or ointment to, especially in religious ceremony

archetype—original model

audacious—bold or daring

balkanized—to break up into small, mutually hostile political units

banal—trite, commonplace

buxom—full-bosomed; plump and healthy looking

cohesion—the act or state of sticking together

consecrate—make sacred

convoy—a group of vehicles traveling together or under escort

cosmology—the science or theory of the universe

credence—belief as to the truth of something

crescendo—a gradual increase in force, volume, or loudness

de facto—existing in actual fact, though not by law

denude—to make bare or naked; to strip

diminutive—remarkably small or tiny

discern—to perceive clearly with the mind or senses

dowry—property or money brought by a bride to her husband

elephantiasis—gross enlargement of the body, especially the limbs, due to lymphatic obstruction by the nematode parasite

empathy—identifying with or vicariously experiencing the feelings, thoughts, or attitudes of another person

ethnomusicology—the study of folk and primitive music and their relation to the cultures to which they belong

eulogy—a speech or writing in praise of a person, especially a deceased person

galvanize—to stimulate, rouse, stir

haint—spirit or ghost
imbue—inspire or permeate with feelings, opinions, or qualities
ingenuous—innocent, open, frank
juxtapose—place side by side
lithography—a process of producing an image on a plate so treated that it is absorbed and printed with special inks
malaise—a vague feeling of physical discomfort or uneasiness; a vague awareness of moral or social decline
Manichean—referring to a theological doctrine of conflict between light and dark
manifest—to make clear or obvious to the eye or mind
monolith—a single block of stone; something having a uniform, massive, or intractable character
nuance—slight variation in tone, color, or meaning
oligarchy—government ruled by a few persons
pantheon—the realm of the heroes or persons venerated by any group
parochial—restricted to a small area or scope; narrow; limited
persecute—to subject to hostile or ill treatment
pickaninny—pejorative term for a black child
pirouette—a dancer's spin on one foot or the point of the toe
plantain—a starchy banana-like fruit used mostly for cooking
plutocracy—government ruled by the wealthy
pontificate—to speak in a pompous or dogmatic manner
portico—a roof supported by columns, usually attached to a building as a porch
predominant—being the strongest element
presage—to portend, foreshadow, or predict
protocol—the customs concerning formality and etiquette
protract—prolong or lengthen in space or especially time
pulverize—to crush or grind into powder or dust
purvey—to provide, furnish, or supply, especially as a business
rapacious—taking by force; plundering
repartee—skill or wit in quick reply
requisite—required, necessary for some purpose
resilient—springing back, resuming original shape
resurrect—to bring back to life
reverberate—to reecho or resound

ribald—coarsely or disrespectfully humorous

scythe—a mowing and reaping implement with a long curved blade swung over the ground

sedition—conduct or speech inciting rebellion

syncopate—shifting of the normal accent in a musical passage, usually by stressing the normally unaccented beats

testimonial—written or unwritten declaration of character, esteem, or qualifications

transcendent—going beyond ordinary limits

trilobite—any marine arthropod of the extinct group Trilobita from the Paleozoic era

undulate—to have or cause a wavy motion

vehemence—forceful, ardent; characterized by anger

voluptuous—characterized by indulgence in pleasure; sensually pleasing or delightful

xenophobia—fear or hatred of strangers, foreigners, or anything foreign

Further Reading

Allen, Ray. *Singing in the Spirit: African-American Sacred Quartets in New York City.* Philadelphia: University of Pensylvania Press, 1991. *Nonfiction*: Explores African-American folk and popular music in New York and around the United States.

Angelou, Maya. *I Know Why the Caged Bird Sings.* New York: Bantam Books, 1988. *Nonfiction*: The autobiography of the celebrated African-American writer and poet.

Bearden, Romaire, and Henderson, Harry. *A History of African-American Artists. Nonfiction*: Examines the lives and careers of more than 50 artists and the relation of their work to artistic, social, and political trends around the world.

Black, Gary J. *My Friend the Gullah.* Columbia, SC: The R. L. Bryan Co., 1993. *Nonfiction*: A recounting of experiences with the Gullah Negroes, residents of the Sea Islands who are descendants of African slaves brought to the South Carolina coast.

Boggs, Vernon W. *Salsiology: Afro-Cuban Music and the Evolution of Salsa in New York City.* New York: Excelsior Music Publishing, 1992. *Nonfiction*: Traces the evolution of salsa from its roots.

Brown, Wesley, and Ling, Amy, eds. *Visions of America: Personal Narratives from the Promised Land.* New York: Persea Books, 1993. *Nonfiction*: Personal essays and autobiographies explore specific tensions of being American with roots in another culture.

Conniff, Michael L., and Davis, Thomas J. *Africans in the Americas: A History of the Black Diaspora.* New York: St Martin's Press, 1994. *Nonfiction*: A history of Africa and the slave trade. Explores life, labor, emancipation, and assimilation in Brazil, the Caribbean, North America and South America.

Daise, Ronald. *Reminiscences of Sea Island Heritage: Legacy of Freedmen on St. Helena Island.* Orangeburg, SC:

Sandlapper Publishing, 1986. *Nonfiction*: Lifestyles, customs, superstitions, and folklore of these first freedmen and their descendants

Debey, Francis, and Bennett, Josephine (trans.). *African Music: A People's Art*. New York: Lawrence Hill Books, 1975. *Nonfiction*: Explores the roots of African music.

Gould, Philip, and Ancelet, Barry Jean. *Cajun Music and Zydeco*. Baton Rouge: Louisiana State University Press, 1993. *Nonfiction*: Collection of photographs of the Cajun and Zydeco community in Louisiana spanning ten years.

Ellison, Ralph. *Invisible Man*. New York: Vintage Books, 1980. *Fiction*: The story of a young African-American who travels from the deep South to Harlem in the 1950s.

Guillermoprieto, Alma. *Samba*. New York: Vintage Books, 1990. *Nonfiction*: An anecdotal narrative examining the history and culture of black Brazilians.

Jones, LeRoi. *Dutchman and The Slave*. New York: Morrow Quill Paperbacks, 1964. *Drama*: The struggle for African-American identity in the twentieth century.

Lomax, Allen. *The Land Where the Blues Began*. New York: Pantheon Books, 1993. *Nonfiction*: An exploration of the harsh origins of the blues.

Major, Clarence. *Juba to Jive: A Dictionary of African-American Slang*. New York: Viking, 1994. *Nonfiction*: This dictionary includes citations, linguistic roots, geographical locations, and dates.

Morrison, Tony. *Beloved*. New York: Plume, 1987. *Fiction*: Protagonist escapes from slavery and is haunted by slavery's legacy.

Murphy, Larry G.; Melton, Gordon; and Ward, Gary L., eds. *Encyclopedia of African American Religions*. New York: Garland, 1993. *Nonfiction*: Articles about religious beliefs explain the significance and context of different traditions.

Naylor, Gloria. *Mama Day*. New York: Vintage Books, 1988. *Fiction*: A generational saga of a postslavery Georgia island community.

Oliver, Paul. *Blues Fell This Morning: Meaning in the Blues*. Cambridge: Cambridge University Press, 1990. *Nonfiction*: A study of the themes, backgrounds, imagery of, and motivation behind the blues.

Oliver, Roland, and Fage, J. D. *A Short History of Africa*. New York: Facts on File, 1988. *Nonfiction*: Explores a rich and previously little-known heritage.

Roberts, John Storm. *Black Music of Two Worlds*. New York: Original Music, 1972. *Nonfiction*: An introduction to African-inspired music on both sides of the Atlantic.

Tate, Greg. *Flyboy in the Buttermilk: Essays on Contemporary America*. New York: Simon & Schuster, 1992. *Nonfiction*: In a collection of essays, this social commentator discusses the cultural significance of a wide variety of subjects.

Thomson, Robert Farris. *Flash of the Spirit*. New York: Vintage Books, 1983. *Nonfiction*: The author shows how five African civilizations have informed and are reflected in the different facets of African American culture in the United States.

———. Face of the Gods. New York: The Museum for African Art, 1993. Nonfiction: Discussion of the altars of African religions and their counterparts in the African Diaspora society in the Americas.

Three Negro Classics. New York: Avon Books, 1965. *Nonfiction*: An anthology of the writings of Booker T. Washington, W. E. B. DuBois, and James Weldon Johnson.

Wexler, Jerry, and Ritz, David. *Rhythm and the Blues: A Life in American Music*. New York: Knopf, 1993. *Nonfiction*: A cultural history of the blues.

Index

165

Index

Harris, Middleton, 124
Harvard University, 159, 161
Hendrix, Jimi, 60
herbs, studying, 149
heritage, African, 57
Heschel, Abraham Joshua, 165
history, sense of, 160-163
    tragic, 161, 164
Hofstadter, Richard, 158
hope, audacious, 165-166
Howard University, 57, 58
Hughes, Robert, 73

I
Iemanjá, 87-100
intellect vs. intelligence, 158
International Afrikan American Ballet, 60, 62, 65

J
Jacob, Max, 81
James, Henry, 160
James, William, 166
jogo-de-capoeira, 17, 18
Johnson, Charles S., 124
Jung, Carl, 79

L
Lollis, Mary Lou, 103-119
Louisiana Territory, 131-144
Lovejoy, Elijah, 161

M
Malcolm X, 165
Malraux, André, 73
Mardi Gras Indians, 138-144
market culture, 166-167
martial arts, 15-28
Matisse, Henri, 81
mermaid, goddess as, 89-100
Mississippi River, 132-133
Mitchell, Mitch, 60
Montana, Big Chief "Tootie," 141, 142
Moraes, Mestre, 26
moral vision, 163
Moreira, Wilson, 87
music
    African, 145-153
    Black Indians', 142-143
    in capoeira, 17-18
    Native American, 134

N
nationalism, 163
Native Americans, 15, 89, 133-144
Negroes, free, 40, 47
New Orleans, 131-144
New York, 57-70
n'golo, 15-16, 21
nigger, as racial epithet, 6-7

O
Oberlin College, 57, 59
Olokun, 59
oral history, 103-119, 125
Orisha, 63, 64, 69
orixás (deities), 87, 89, 90
Otis, Johnny, 124

P
Parks, Rosa, 161
Pascal, Blaise, 157, 167
Pastinha, Mestre Vincente, 16, 20, 21-22, 26
Peirce, Charles Sanders, 165
Pequeno, Mestre João, 24
Picasso, Pablo, 73, 79,81
Plessy v. Ferguson decision, 137
Power, the, 63, 65, 69, 70
public life, regeneration of, 157-168

R
race, aspects of, 159-166
racism, in US South, 112-114
rhythm, 145-153
ritual
    Native American, 133
    performance as, 61-62

S
Schecter, William, 123
Schneckenberger, Manfred, 74
Scott, Dred, 50-51
sculpture, African, 57, 73, 74, 82
segregation, 115
self-criticism, 164-165
Shango, 59, 64, 66
slavery
    abolition of
        in Brazil, 16
        in Louisiana, 132-133
    Natchez sold into, 134
    origin of game in, 124
    skit about, 4

166